Praise

With a web of cunning characters and their murky pasts, one never knows whom to trust in *Oxford Soju Club*. Jinwoo Park's clever debut offers a fresh and propulsive examination of Korean identity.
— EDDY BOUDEL TAN, author of *After Elias* and *The Rebellious Tide*

A tangled trident of three intense storylines, *Oxford Soju Club* is more than a spy thriller. Exploring the limits of nationality, loyalty, and race, Jinwoo Park's debut invites important conversations surrounding Korean diasporic identity and belonging in a modern geopolitical world obsessed with national security.
— JAMIE CHAI YUN LIEW, bestselling author of *Dandelion*

Jinwoo Park's *Oxford Soju Club* takes you over like music, immediate and eventually obsessive, the sort of book you cheat on your work with, the one you slip away to read. Sentence for sentence, the prose is a fine thread winding through this game of spies, and eventually you realize the thread also winds through you. And this is because Park is not just a master but an enchanter.
— ALEXANDER CHEE, author of *How to Write an Autobiographical Novel* and *The Queen of the Night*

Oxford Soju Club is an astute examination of identity, diaspora, and longing cleverly masquerading as a spy thriller. Against the backdrop of political intrigue and covert espionage, Jinwoo Park peels back the layers on the many masks immigrants and those with multiple identities must contend with to form a kaleidoscopic picture of what it means to be Korean in today's modern world.
— KARISSA CHEN, author of *Homeseeking*

Jinwoo Park's *Oxford Soju Club* would be right at home amongst the works of Herron and le Carré with its tight turns of plot and thoughtfully considered lingo. But on top of crafting a clever spy thriller, Park uses its vernacular of shifting alliances, donned masks, and the training one undergoes to assimilate to deftly probe questions of diasporic identity and how we decide where we belong. Sly, ingenious, and profoundly felt — I loved it.

— ELAINE U. CHO, author of *Ocean's Godori*

Wildly inventive, fast-paced, and glowing with heart, *Oxford Soju Club* is an unforgettable debut. A spy thriller interlacing the paths of three individuals embroiled in what threatens to become an international incident, this book stayed with me long after I'd finished it, not only for its breakneck plot but also the poignant way it describes trying to exist between worlds and to carve a place of your own in between. Jinwoo Park has a lifelong reader in me.

— Jinwoo Chong, author of *Flux*

Oxford Soju Club ingeniously transposes the code-switching and shape-shifting that diasporic Asians experience in the English-speaking world into a twisty, tension-filled spy story. A writer of great promise, Jinwoo Park navigates issues of identity as effortlessly as he transcends genre.

— KEVIN CHONG, author of *The Double Life of Benson Yu*

Jinwoo Park's deftly crafted spy novel of desperate allegiances has the weight of national as well as personal tragedy. Northerner, Southerner, Westerner, spy — conflicting identities cast long shadows onto history in each character's struggle to survive. What a great read.

— ANTON HUR, author of *Toward Eternity*

Oxford Soju Club is an intelligent, riveting, and poignant exploration asking, "What makes you who you are?" and "Do you determine your own identity?" It's a novel full of yearning, like the eponymous drink — but also, ultimately, of hope.

— JUHEA KIM, author of *Beasts of a Little Land* and *City of Night Birds*

Oxford Soju Club is a gripping spy thriller that, at its core, tackles fundamental questions of identity and our place in the world. Park writes with stark honesty, deftly unravelling the inner turmoil of those caught between duty and self. A wonderful debut.

— MONIKA KIM, author of *The Eyes Are the Best Part*

Fast-moving and dexterous, *Oxford Soju Club* is an innovative espionage story that exposes the boundaries of assimilation, diaspora, and loyalty and what we do to survive.

— LISA KO, author of *Memory Piece*

A fascinating, genre-shifting debut shaped as much by the twists and turns of espionage as by the pull of diasporic longing. I read *Oxford Soju Club* in one sitting, gripped by Jinwoo Park's ingenious evoking of a world I didn't want to leave.

— R.O. KWON, author of *Exhibit*

Jinwoo Park's debut is sharp and evocative, conjuring Oxford's moody cobblestones and shadowed alleyways with cinematic clarity. The pacing is expertly calibrated, balancing kinetic action with contemplative depth. His reimagining of the spy novel favours psychological tension over bombast, more le Carré than Bond, yet distinctly infused with the emotional gravity of diaspora narratives. It recalls the introspective weight of Viet Thanh Nguyen's *The Sympathizer* and the emotional resonance of Celeste Ng's *Everything I Never Told You*. *Oxford Soju Club* marks Jinwoo Park as a literary voice to watch. This kicks the doors open for other Korean diasporic writers, while raising the bar for genre-bending fiction that is as thrilling as it is thought-provoking. The spy craft will make you quickly turn the pages, but the richly crafted characters will linger well after the final page — a haunting, intelligent, and resonant read.

— WAYNE NG, award-winning author of *Johnny Delivers*

A subtle and quiet portrayal of the intersubjectivity of diasporic life told through the form of a spy thriller. Espionage is used to put forward the anxieties of living in the in-between space of needing to be accepted in new cultural contexts and of feeling like the place you once thought was home no longer needs you. At once thrilling and complex, Jinwoo Park's *Oxford Soju Club* gives narrative to life experiences that leave echoes in our bodies but feel too convoluted to articulate clearly. In this small bar in Oxford, where the lives of spies, CIA agents, and immigrants cross, the histories and feelings of these diasporic bodies are given voice.

— SHEUNG-KING, author of *Batshit Seven*

Spare in style but elaborate in design, *Oxford Soju Club* is both a classic tale of spy versus spy and a deep meditation on Korean immigrant identity. Through an intricate cast of characters, this penetrating debut novel asks how each of us might shed our assigned aliases and throw ourselves into "the waves of life." Jinwoo Park is a writer to watch.

— JACK WANG, author of the award-winning *We Two Alone*

Oxford Soju Club glitters with ferocious intelligence and propulsive action, as it is both a fast-paced spy thriller and disarming exploration of the Korean diaspora. With bold confidence, Park offers readers a fresh and cerebral perspective that explores the existential and physical unmooring of three very disparate characters. Asian diasporic literature is often reduced to stereotypes, tropes, and trauma, but Park skillfully reinvents the genre with his masterful storytelling and meticulous prose. The novel's themes are certainly dark, but this is a highly original and page-turning tale that grapples with the thornier aspects of identity, loyalty, duty, patriotism, and survival in perilous times.

— LINDSAY WONG, author of *The Woo-Woo* and *Tell Me Pleasant Things about Immortality*

OXFORD SOJU CLUB

OXFORD SOJU CLUB

a novel

DUNDURN PRESS

Jinwoo Park

Copyright © Jinwoo Park, 2025

All rights reserved. No part of this publication may be reproduced, stored in a retrieval system, or transmitted in any form or by any means, electronic, mechanical, photocopying, recording, or otherwise (except for brief passages for purpose of review) without the prior permission of Dundurn Press. Permission to photocopy should be requested from Access Copyright.

All characters in this work are fictitious. Any resemblance to real persons, living or dead, is purely coincidental.

Publisher: Meghan Macdonald | Acquiring editor: Julia Kim
Cover design and illustration: Laura Boyle

Library and Archives Canada Cataloguing in Publication

Title: Oxford Soju Club: a novel / Jinwoo Park.
Names: Park, Jinwoo, author.
Identifiers: Canadiana (print) 20240478509 | Canadiana (ebook) 20240478517 | ISBN 9781459755109 (softcover) | ISBN 9781459755116 (PDF) | ISBN 9781459755123 (EPUB)
Subjects: LCGFT: Thrillers (Fiction) | LCGFT: Spy fiction. | LCGFT: Novels.
Classification: LCC PS8631.A74796 O94 2025 | DDC C813/.6—dc23

We acknowledge the support of the Canada Council for the Arts and the Ontario Arts Council for our publishing program. We also acknowledge the financial support of the Government of Ontario, through the Ontario Book Publishing Tax Credit and Ontario Creates, and the Government of Canada.

Care has been taken to trace the ownership of copyright material used in this book. The author and the publisher welcome any information enabling them to rectify any references or credits in subsequent editions.

The publisher is not responsible for websites or their content unless they are owned by the publisher.

Printed and bound in Canada.

Dundurn Press
1382 Queen Street East
Toronto, Ontario, Canada M4L 1C9
dundurn.com, @dundurnpress

*To the family I was born to,
and the family that I chose.*

CHAPTER 1

The Northerner

YOHAN FINDS DOHA STABBED IN AN ALLEYWAY BARELY wide enough for two people. At first he thinks it is not too late to save him. He turns his head to check for an attacker as he crouches down to where Doha is slumped on the ground. He has been stabbed in the abdomen. Underneath Doha's coat blood soaks his white shirt a deep crimson. The knife cut into where he would be guaranteed to bleed out.

As Yohan reaches to open Doha's coat wider, he feels a hand on his wrist, and he looks up to find Doha's eyes open. The grip is weak, but it gradually tightens as Doha puts all his remaining strength into his hand. Doha's eyes lock on Yohan's with a kind of intense gaze Yohan has never seen from Doha before.

"Yohan-a," he says in Korean, which makes Yohan pause. It has been a while since he has heard him speak their own language. "I told you to stay back at the flat."

By instinct Yohan wants to apologize for his insubordination, but he knows such words are meaningless. He glances down at the flowing blood, takes out a handkerchief from his pants pocket, and puts it to the wound. It becomes drenched immediately.

"Don't bother," Doha says, noticing Yohan's brewing desperation. "I don't have long. So listen carefully now. Everything depends on this." He pauses to breathe and winces a few times as he grips where the knife went in. "Soju Club. You know the place."

Yohan nods.

"That's where she'll find you."

"Dr. Ryu? She's coming there?"

"She has a plan. To get you away from the Americans, the South Koreans, from everyone."

"She's coming tonight? Tomorrow?"

"Soju Club, Dr. Ryu," Doha whispers, his breathing getting more ragged.

"Commander Doha, please, when is she coming?"

"She'll find you. Just wait. She'll come for you when the time is right. Yohan. Yohan-a."

Doha keeps saying Yohan's name, unable to continue but wanting to speak. His trembling hands try reaching for him, but he lacks the strength to do so. Yohan leans in and puts Doha's bloodied palm to his cheek, feeling the damp smear on his skin.

"Live. Yohan-a. Live."

With these words a trail of dark red trickles down from one end of Doha's mouth to his chin. His head falls slightly to the side, but his eyes remain on Yohan, who looks back as it hits him. Doha is dead.

The first thing he must do is to remove Doha's identification. The protocol is to render anyone left behind unidentifiable by their pursuers, whether it is the dogged Southerners or the meddlesome westerners. He digs through the inside pocket of Doha's coat, pulls out his wallet, and quickly retreats from the alley, leaving the body behind. He weaves through residential streets, his senses fully alert to spot anything out of order. The roads are empty. The houses are dark.

When Yohan returns to their flat, he gathers passports and other documents that could implicate Doha. He shoves it all, including his own papers, into a backpack. Once the place has been cleaned of their trace, Yohan hurries back onto the street, his eyes efficiently scanning his surroundings. The city sleeps early, and no one is out at this time of night. He must be on the move constantly and create as many variables as possible to keep whoever is tracking him guessing.

Soju Club, Dr. Ryu. Yohan repeats Doha's last order to himself.

By this time the restaurant would be closed. It is not too far away, just across the bridge on Cowley Road, sitting amongst narrow buildings, flanked by flats on either side. He throws a glance over his shoulder as he strolls down the neatly tiled sidewalk, watching for a lone stalker. When he stops at a crossing, he looks to his right, where a car brakes only a metre or two away from him. It is a green sedan with a middle-aged occupant looking straight ahead and waiting for the light. Yohan breathes in and anticipates for the door to open, a gun emerging and blasting off in his direction. His hands tense. If he acts quickly, he can close the distance. But just as he thinks about making a move on the car, the light changes and the driver continues down the road. Yohan feels the tension seeping out of him and exhales.

When he crosses the bridge onto Cowley, he notices a pair of bright headlights behind him, cutting through the night.

Instead of going to his destination, he crosses the street and enters a corner store. He browses the aisles and as he looks back to check the street, the car passes by the door. He buys an energy drink, steps outside, and cracks it open, drinking it in small slurps. Standing in front of the store, he looks directly at the sign across the street. In big white cursive letters, Soju Club declares itself just above its windows. It opens at eleven in the morning, but the owner usually appears around six to start his day.

Yohan crosses the road and looks in the windows. The restaurant is unlit and deserted. He can see chairs upside down on top of tables. There is a fridge near the cash register; he can see the green tint of soju bottles illuminated by the cooler's light. He sees nothing unusual from the hundreds of other times he has been here in the past.

He takes a pin from his pocket, picks the lock, and opens the glass door. In the darkness of the empty restaurant, he pulls down two chairs from a table where he and Doha used to drink together. He sits at one end and looks across to the empty seat where Doha is supposed to be. It doesn't quite feel right, so he goes over to the cooler and pulls out a bottle along with two chilled shot glasses resting on the bottom shelf. He pours two shots — one for himself and another for Doha.

Yohan tries to say something, a word or two that will honour Doha, perhaps, or a burning question that he didn't have the chance to ask the commander while he was still alive. Nothing seems appropriate, so he silently brings his shot glass in contact with the glass resting on Doha's side of the table. He drinks in his memory. That is all Yohan can do for him now.

He considers finishing the bottle, but he wants his mind to stay clear. He pours the rest down the sink and puts the chairs back up on the table. He locks up the front and exits through the back because he knows it's the only door that locks automatically. Once he is in the back alley, he deposits the bottle into a nearby trash can and disappears into the narrow streets, warily looking around in anticipation of a pursuer.

•

On their first day in Oxford, they do nothing but walk around. Doha calls it reconnaissance. Yohan follows. This is something Dr. Ryu emphasized — he is to always follow Doha's directions and to never question him.

After they cross Magdalen Bridge, Yohan registers all the street names: St. Clement's, Cowley, and Iffley. They stroll down Cowley, Doha with his two hands folded behind his back and Yohan prepared to act if the need arises. He hasn't been able to loosen up since they landed in Bern three days ago. At every train station, every hotel, his eyes are busy, watching and learning.

"You're too tense," Doha says in English. He stops abruptly, prompting Yohan to stop as well.

"I'm sorry," Yohan says.

"No need to be sorry. Just relax a bit. There's no need to be vigilant here. This is as safe as it gets for us."

"Dr. Ryu said —"

"What she said was for the sake of the Bureau and for those who may be listening. Out here it's just me and you."

"She said our enemies are watching us."

"So they watch us," Doha says, leaning back with his arms open. "What would they do? Kill us? What would be the point of that? They would learn nothing from our deaths. You see, the people we consider as our enemies are rational. They don't act unless they want something."

"What would that be?"

"Information. These people thrive on knowing. They are careful surveyors of risk, which guides all their actions. Too much risk, they don't act. Too little risk, they'll be suspicious. They want the right amount of risk, where the balance of consequence and benefit is equal. And if they believe we hold certain pieces of the puzzle, they'll come for us then. But for now, they'll watch from afar. And they'll do nothing." Yohan wants to ask how he is so certain, but he reminds himself that Doha has been doing this for longer than he has been alive. It was Doha who got him into the program, and as much as he has Dr. Ryu to thank for raising him and educating him, Doha is the reason why he was chosen to be here. He knows how important and prestigious all this is and that he is here to fulfill the great purpose of serving the Leader. Doha starts walking again and Yohan obediently trails after him.

"What do we do when they come for us?"

"Don't you worry. When the time comes, I'll tell you what to do, and all you need to do is follow my orders."

Doha stops suddenly, looks to his right, and exclaims that they have finally arrived. Puzzled, Yohan looks and sees that it's a restaurant. Above the door is a sign that reads "Soju Club." Doha goes inside and Yohan follows. Doha seems at ease with the place, drifting to a table as if it is his own designated spot. Yohan joins him, looking around. There are no patrons. A man emerges from behind the counter, drying his hands on his apron as he walks over to them, a friendly look on his face.

The first thing Yohan notices is how the man's face is devoid of wrinkles. The man is youthful, his skin taut, marked only by the scant acne on his cheeks.

"That's the owner," Doha says.

"He's young."

"Almost as young as you, I believe."

The restaurant owner briskly steps toward the table, handing them menus. "Greetings," he says in English with a Korean accent. "Hello, sir! You're back," he says to Doha, who nods with a grin.

"Well, I had to show this young man here the most wonderful Korean restaurant I know in town," Doha says, his hands gesturing toward Yohan. "He just arrived here today."

"Are you visiting?"

As he had practised with Dr. Ryu at the academy back in Pyongyang, Yohan recites the details of his alias. The life that he is supposed to lead. "I'm actually a graduate student here."

"And where are you from?"

"From Nantes."

"Nantes. Where is that?"

"France."

"You're from France? But you are —" The owner pauses, tipping his head and then looking slightly embarrassed.

"I was born in France, but my parents are Japanese."

"Ah, Japanese," he says, nodding in comprehension. "Well, I hope you like Korean food." He sounds genuine.

Yohan cannot help smiling. "I'm sure I will," he answers.

Doha names a few items without looking at the menu. Sundubu jjigae, jeyuk bokkeum, and a pajeon to share.

"That was good, Junichi. Very smooth. I see that the conversation training has paid off," Doha says as the owner goes to the counter to enter the orders.

Only a day ago, he was Yiwei Xi from Shandong. He has already wiped the memory of that fictional person to make space for the French-born Japanese graduate student Junichi Nakamura, hailing from Nantes, now studying at the University of Oxford.

The Southerner

Jihoon brakes just short of the curb in front of his restaurant. He takes his helmet off and ties his thin-framed bicycle to a street sign. The day always starts for him at six in the morning, leaving him a good head start before opening at eleven, and he needs all the prep time he can get with only one employee coming later. Even when he doesn't get enough sleep, he sticks to the schedule because a good work ethic is valuable no matter what — one of the many lessons his mother had passed down to him.

Darkness still looms outside. A few office workers are walking toward the city centre. A lone lorry bounces along, squeaking and clattering. Jihoon breathes in the cool damp air, and once he feels ready, he turns around and walks inside. The first thing he does after hanging up his jacket is start the coffee machine. Under bright fluorescent lights in the kitchen, he fills a large pot with water. He guts dried anchovies of their blackened insides and puts them into the pot along with sheets of brittle kelp and the ends of green onions. The anchovy broth will be used for practically all the stews on the menu, sundubu jjigae being one of the most sought after. Just then the coffee machine beeps, telling him it is ready. He pours himself a cup and steps back outside.

Across from his restaurant is an off-licence convenience store, run by a plump middle-aged Pakistani man whose belly hangs around him like a tire. The man is sweeping the pavement in front of his shop. He looks up, sees Jihoon holding coffee, and waves. Jihoon waves back. They have been waving at each other for the past several years, since Jihoon opened his place. They still do not know each other's names.

The Soju Club is the only Korean restaurant in the city, and that alone is a draw for many. When he first stepped foot in Oxford, he found it strangely empty, particularly in comparison to Seoul, Busan, or even Sacheon, the seaside town his mother is from. Back in Seoul there would be three fried chicken places, five noraebangs, six Korean barbeque joints, and even two plastic surgery offices, all in one block. From what he saw, Oxford had no buildings higher than three storeys. The transit was inconvenient at best and, on an average day, frustrating enough to induce cancer, as his mother would often say when irritated. All of it — the buildings, the people, the pubs that close at midnight, and the gift shops selling T-shirts with "Oxford" proudly printed on them — is less of a city and more of a town. Somewhere in the middle.

With the coffee mug in one hand, Jihoon steps farther out and lights a cigarette. The habit started when he came to Oxford to open his restaurant with a pack of cigarettes from home. Jihoon smoked the pack within a week, and he started craving more. He tried local brands, but he missed the smoothness of ones from home. Now he orders cartons of Korean cigarettes through a website.

These early morning smokes are the best, when there is barely anyone on the street. It's just him, his cigarette, and the city in a calm reverie. A single strand of smoke dances up to the streetlights. He looks at the shallow step that leads to the door of the Soju Club, where the professor was standing yesterday. The professor had always come with his student, a young French-born

Japanese man from Nantes. Jihoon thought the younger man was an odd mixture of identities, and it is a wonder to him. Where you are born, whom you are born to, and the way you are raised — these used to be trivial details. Jihoon never thought about such things when he was in Korea, a country with only one kind of people, the Korean kind. Now Jihoon wonders how the student feels, to be such a puzzle of a person. He wonders if he speaks any Japanese. He has only heard him talk in English, whether it was to order or to chat with the professor.

The professor came alone last night, without the student. Jihoon had just finished his cigarette outside when the professor stepped out, asking for one. Jihoon took two out, one for the professor and one for himself, so that the professor wouldn't smoke alone.

"This is good. What brand is it?" the professor asked.

"THIS."

"Yes, this cigarette, what is it called?"

"THIS."

When he saw the professor's face curl up in confusion, Jihoon showed him the pack with the word "THIS" clearly visible.

"THIS," he said. "I see. You got it from Korea? You went there recently?"

"No, I get them shipped to Oxford. I haven't gone back in a while."

"Ah, really? Why's that?"

Jihoon found this question strange, that this professor, who regarded their relationship only as one of patronage, would suddenly be so interested in him.

"It just didn't feel right. I felt this constant grip in my chest. Like the air you breathe chokes you instead."

Jihoon didn't know why he said it in such a way. Perhaps it was the evening lull, when all the thoughts of home and his mother he had ignored were trying to clamber over the wall he had built around his mind.

"I feel the same," the professor said to him. "I never felt at home back in my country. It's a funny thing. To be told that you belong somewhere and feel nothing for it. That's why I don't feel like going back ever. I'm fine here. I'm not saying Oxford is home either. It just feels better, I guess. Like you said."

"And where's home for you?"

"Same as you."

"Korea?"

The professor nodded. "Seoul, right?" he asked.

Jihoon stopped in the middle of putting his cigarette back to his mouth, the filter hovering at his lips. "Yes," he answered.

"But you were born in Sacheon, on the southern coast."

"Yes," Jihoon said, trying to recall if he had ever revealed this detail to the professor.

"Raised by your mother, your father an absent figure."

Jihoon did not respond.

"It's okay. Me too," he said.

Before Jihoon could respond, the professor threw his spent cigarette to the ground. "It's been a pleasure eating and drinking at the Soju Club, Im Jihoon-ssi," he said in Korean before he turned to walk down the street.

After he has had the opportunity to sleep on it, Jihoon has many questions about the strange encounter. More than the fact that the professor knew details of his birthplace and his father, it is the way he said his name that lingers. He has only ever heard "Jihoon Lim" since coming to Oxford, never "Lim Jihoon," or "Im Jihoon" for that matter, the Korean way of saying it.

He stares down the sidewalk of Cowley Road and mutters the name just like how the professor said it. "Im Jihoon." He wants to feel something, like when he was surprised by the discovery that the professor knew so much about his life. Nothing comes to him.

•

The nights stretch into long hours, and she always stays later than him. He needs to go home and study for his exams, though he wants to stay longer. There is not enough time to do everything he needs to do.

This is their restaurant. Their livelihood. A little corner of Seoul that Jihoon and his mother have managed to secure for themselves. When they came from Sacheon, escaping an abusive alcoholic man, he was only a child, still small enough for her to carry when she snuck out with a cloth sack tied to her back, accompanied by just enough money to catch a bus to Seoul. They stayed with one of her uncles, who was a construction worker. It was a cramped affair, but they managed because the alternative was going back, and that was unthinkable.

Jihoon's mother found herself working odd jobs, like serving in restaurants, cleaning toilets in office buildings, and handing out flyers for stores in the middle of the street. In the evenings Jihoon would return from his after-school study sessions and find his mother pressing cooling patches on her back for pain relief. He would help her by sticking the patches onto hard-to-reach places.

She collected the money she earned very diligently, and from early on, Jihoon understood that every time he saw something he wanted, he could not ask his mother for it. They eventually were able to move into a place of their own, a small apartment in Hapjeong from which the Han River was only a fifteen-minute walk away. The building was old, four storeys with brick walls that didn't exist in new builds. It was a densely crowded neighbourhood with streets barely wide enough to let a car go by and the constant smell of sewage. But it was theirs.

His mother found a small lot squeezed between a grocery store and a dilapidated residential building. It used to be a laundromat, but the owner had passed away and the son was looking to sell. The location was decent. It was at the mouth of a three-way intersection, one of them feeding into a big road. Cars and trucks shoved past each other on one-way streets with couriers on motorcycles weaving in and out. There she set up a tiny restaurant that could barely seat ten people. Hungry and tired workers from the nearby factory would stream in for lunch and dinner. As if their patience was being rewarded, the good fortunes came in repeated waves, and Jihoon and his mother had thought that this was it. They had made it.

Jihoon comes to help as soon as he has finished his day's studies. He started out washing the dishes, then moved on to serving customers and taking orders. Now he even makes the simpler recipes, as well as making sure the big rice cooker is always full of steaming white rice that gleams in any amount of light.

One evening, while washing dishes after the last customer had gone, Jihoon asks his mother a question. "You want to go on a trip, Eomma?"

"A trip?" she answers, focused on drying the dishes that Jihoon has just rinsed.

"Yeah, a trip. It'd be nice. We should take a vacation. Take some time off. You work too hard."

"I work hard for you and that's all I need."

His mother never complained about anything. Study hard, get into a good university, and everything would be fine. There was no need to go anywhere because everything she needed was right here — the restaurant and her son. There was no need to pick things up and go elsewhere. But once he got into a good school, maybe they could take a break together.

"I'm going to be okay. I had a good score on my mock exam. Let's go somewhere after my exams. Come on, Eomma."

She smiles, still looking down at the dishes. Her hands continue wiping them and piling them next to the sink, but Jihoon knows he is getting to her.

"Where would we go?" she asks.

"Where do you want to go?"

"How about Andong? We can go visit all the old houses and eat some jjimdak. That would be nice, right?"

He likes the sound of jjimdak, but he is not satisfied with her answer. He wants her to try again, think bigger. "Why don't we fly somewhere?"

"Like Jeju?"

"No, what I mean is, let's go to another country."

"Another country?"

"Yeah. You know, anywhere. Where would you like to go?"

"I don't know, I don't think it's a good idea," she says, shaking her head. "Plane tickets are expensive. Not to mention all the money we'd be spending while there. It's better to save the money for your tuition. We have to have enough for your university education."

They wash the dishes in silence, until the last of them are done. Jihoon tries to find the opportunity to bring the subject up again, but his mother's stern face tells him that he should not talk about it any longer. As usual his mother shoves him out of the restaurant early, saying that he needs to go home and study.

"I can study here and wait for you," Jihoon says.

"Nonsense. How can you concentrate with me clattering about? Just go home. I'll be there soon."

As he walks away and looks back to his smiling mother, he thinks about how he doesn't particularly want to go to university. He wants to stay with her, in the restaurant, where it's warm and everything makes sense. But he also knows if he said any of that, it would hurt her. So he keeps his mouth shut and walks home alone under the dim streetlights.

The American

It's a disaster. She rushes into the alleyway to find Doha Kim's body leaned against a wall. She measures his pulse at his neck and realizes that he is far gone.

"Shit," she utters. "Oh shit."

The first thing Yunah does is call Thomas, who simply responds with "Wait for me." While she stands by, she looks for any personal items on Doha. His wallet is already gone, and the rest of his pockets turn up empty.

Hearing footsteps, she puts her hand to her hip, but it's Thomas. They ease up upon seeing each other.

"How long?" Thomas asks as he steps over to look at the body.

"It's been recent. Maybe fifteen minutes before I got to him."

Something felt off tonight. Junichi did not show up. CCTV footage caught Doha making a rendezvous with someone by Carfax Tower. She figured it was a routine meeting. He often met with his many friends from the university. But Yunah always looked on the off chance it could be the fabled Dr. Ryu. In the dark she couldn't tell exactly who it was. Short hair, with a black coat. They disappeared into an alleyway. Later, a motorcycle with two people burst out and quickly sped away. Doha never came out. That was when Yunah decided to sprint her way down here, where she discovered Doha's body.

"Let's get him out of here," Yunah says.

They carry him out of the alleyway and onto the street, each holding Doha's body by a shoulder so that it looks like they're just helping a drunk man who passed out, except for the constant dripping of blood onto the ground. Yunah opens the car door, and they throw him into the back seat with a simultaneous grunt. As they drive back to the pub, Thomas turns his head toward Yunah, in the passenger seat, a few times, as if there is something he wants to say. He keeps quiet until they stop at a light.

It has only been two weeks since the death of Kim Jong-il, but Yunah thought they would have more time to bring in Doha. The speed at which the North Koreans moved astounded even veteran observers. Like fire spreading quickly through paper, they were erasing the former regime's traces.

"Do you want to call it in, or should I do it?" Thomas asks.

"No, not yet. Let's find the other guy. He's still out there," Yunah says.

"He's a nobody. A pawn, just a foot soldier. Doha Kim was the only fish that mattered."

"He can still give us names and locations."

"Of what? The dead ones? The burned safe houses? Face it, it's done. They're tying up loose ends. They've finished it with Doha Kim."

"They haven't. He's still out there."

A honk interrupts the argument. The light is green, and Thomas continues to drive down the road. "We're calling it in," he says. "That's it. That's all there's left to do."

Once they are back at the pub, they park by the curb in front. "There are still patrons in there," Thomas says as he turns the car off. "I'll get them out, and then we'll bring his body in."

When Thomas disappears inside, Yunah looks back to the body lying on the back seat, arms limp and stretched over one side, head thrown back and mouth open. If not for the stab wound, he would look like any other passed-out drunk catching a ride home. She can see the slickness of wet blood on the leather seat, dripping down toward the floor of the car. They will have a hell of a time cleaning it off.

As she waits, her mind wanders. There is value with Junichi Nakamura. This much she knows. No ordinary underling would spend so much time with Doha Kim. She has listened in on their conversations. The way they speak to each other — it is not that of a commander and a soldier. There is affection.

She glances up at the sign that says "Magpie" with a drawing of a black-and-white bird. Thomas let her choose the name of the pub, not out of generosity but because he couldn't bother to, and this was what she settled on. When he asked why, she shrugged and said she liked magpies. She didn't think he'd understand that her grandmother used to tell her that for Koreans, the magpie, otherwise called kkachi, is a bird that brings good fortune.

A motorcycle roars past, and when she glances at it, she is shocked that it is the same motorcycle from earlier. A black café racer. It stops not too far away, maybe three car lengths. The helmeted rider looks back at Yunah, and she wonders whether this is a prelude for an ambush. Her left hand palms the sidearm hidden at her hip while her other hand grips the door handle.

They stare at each other in the darkness. Yunah wants to look around, to see if anyone is sneaking up beside the vehicle, but she is afraid that she will lose him if she looks away. Just as she is about to swing the door open, a group of drunk revellers pour out of the pub and cross the road, passing the windshield and blocking her view. When they are gone, the motorcycle is no longer there.

CHAPTER 2

The Northerner

THE PROBLEM IS SIMPLE YET UNRESOLVABLE. HE DOES not know when she will arrive. Only that she will be here soon. The language is ambiguous, unlike his usual commands, which are clearly laid out with regards to time, date, location, and target.

"There will be a time when none of us will be here for you," Doha once said in passing, his soju glass dangling from his fingers, filled to the brim. They were sitting in the Soju Club, as they always did in the evening. "When that time comes, just do one thing. Stay alive. No matter what. Live."

Live. Yohan-a. Live.

He must live, no matter what. He must stay safe and meet with Dr. Ryu. His mind, fogged with sleep deprivation, jolts awake at this reminder. He has no weapon on him. Doha never thought it was important, despite Dr. Ryu's recommendation. His philosophy was that they needed to hide in plain sight. They were here to be part of the civilized world, one in which violence was not the norm but an exception. Dr. Ryu thought this was imprudent, leaving Yohan defenceless, but Doha was adamant.

"Say he has a gun on him. A situation arises and he needs to use it. So what then, pull it out and fire it? Well, now you've woken up the damn neighbourhood. Even if it isn't used, what if he gets noticed, even detained? What sort of a modest foreigner carries a weapon? He needs to be one of them. He needs to speak their language and blend in. To be able to walk these streets without standing out. Even if there is an attacker on his trail, he should be able to go up to a police officer and get help. That's what we are trying to do here."

Instead, the weapon of choice that Doha championed was trust. Trust from law enforcement that he was a good citizen on the surface. Trust from unassuming members of the public that he was a harmless bystander. Trust that could be used to slip into any place or talk to anyone. Dr. Ryu shunned Doha's espionage doctrine for its organic nature. Field missions, in her mind, were all about reliability and risk management. Exposing yourself to someone else was already a security threat. Engaging someone actively was suicide. Trust was a hazard, not a tool.

Doha did not back down from his position and educated Yohan on how to socialize in order to promote trust. Information was best extracted from willing mouths, and for that to happen, you had to get close to someone. "Always be as humble as possible. Lower yourself. People do not trust those who seem better than them. The ego is used to looking down, not up. It is natural for humans to raise their defences and be on their guard when they feel an imbalance. So make sure the odds are stacked in their favour and against yours. Structure your first impressions around that."

Unfortunately, trust cannot protect him from a knife or a bullet. It certainly did not for Doha.

Oxford is empty at this early hour, the sky still dark and the streetlights bright. Yohan looks around as he walks through the narrow avenues lined with houses, as if to invite the enemy from the shadows. He is right here, waiting. But nothing happens. He is alone, and Oxford, which seemed so small compared to other places, feels as if it is about to engulf him.

Soju Club, Dr. Ryu.

It sounds to him more like a prayer than an order now. Something to calm his nerves, a reminder that there is still some sense of rationale in what he is doing, that he is not simply lost in aimless wander.

He returns to the spot where he found Doha. There is a sign that reads "Clarks Row" and a CCTV camera pointed right at the mouth of the alley. He goes down the narrow pathway, past the slight bend that is concealed from the CCTV, and stops where Doha was murdered. Someone has moved the body. He sees a dried pool of blood on the cobblestones. If Doha was being chased, he would have stayed in sight of the cameras. He was never reckless. This was planned carefully. Doha had agreed to meet someone here.

"Remember, your identity is your strongest weapon. Forget who you are. Yohan Kim is no good here. But Junichi Nakamura, he is part of the world. This society. Our work must be done in the light, not in the shadows, so that everything is seen and heard. Because our enemies prefer the shadows, where they can do their dirty work in secret. But if we're out here, walking freely about, then that poses a risk for them. We force them to bring out their shady affairs in public. To be seen is to be safe."

Yohan goes back to the conversation they had at the Soju Club last week.

"In three days there's a meeting," Doha said.

"Meeting with whom? Are we being extracted?"

"Details will be discussed at the meeting."

"Where will it be held?"

"You're not coming with me. I'm going by myself. You'll stay at the flat."

Yohan did not understand the directive. He blinked repeatedly as he tried to mask his confusion.

"Why?"

"Because I said so."

"It's not safe on your own."

"I decide what is safe or not. I give the orders. And the order is that you stay at the flat while I handle this."

Yohan had never thought of talking back to Doha like this before, but times were extraordinary. "Commander, please. Ever since the regime change, they're not answering us and we're being left in the dark. I have to think we're being wiped out. What if they're trying to draw you out? I have to be there to protect you."

"You are wrong," Doha said sternly, folding his arms onto the table. "I am the one protecting you. I always have and I always will. I need you to listen to me. I have never led you astray. You trust me, right?"

Yohan could only nod.

"Good. After I return from the meeting, it'll be better. There'll be a way out."

But Yohan was right in the end. Doha had been crossed off. Yohan is likely next, and what he does from here on out will be critical to staying alive until Dr. Ryu arrives.

"If you're ever in a situation where there is no escape, go to the Americans," Doha taught him. "Stay close to them. Grab them by their belt buckles if you have to."

"Why the Americans?" Yohan had asked.

"They're plotters. They always weigh each decision carefully. They always care about being smart, about making the right moves that benefit them. They are driven by self-interest, and that gives rise to a certain degree of predictability."

"Predictable how?"

"Their loyalty is conditional, whereas our loyalty is unconditional and completely irrational. We could be having lunch with a best friend and *bang*, bullet through the eye, just because we were ordered to."

"How are you so sure?"

"It's not in their blood. It's not in them to unconditionally follow orders. They can't help but think for themselves. They'll try to make sense of it, try to see what's in it for them. It's ironic in a way. A nation full of individuals all wanting to go their own way somehow builds the world's most powerful union. That's them, the Americans."

Yohan makes up his mind. He'll stay close to the Americans for now, see what they do, and if necessary, find an opportunity to communicate with them. He walks east, back toward the Soju Club. He crosses Magdalen Bridge, continues down to the fork, then turns onto Cowley Road, walking until he sees the entrance to the Magpie. The lights are off, which makes sense since it is far past closing time. But the lights of the flat above the pub are lit. Seonhye is still awake.

Yohan wonders if he should try to see her. Talk to her perhaps. But as of now, he can't be Junichi Nakamura, the man who visits Seonhye the bartender every night. That game is on pause, and the masks have to come off temporarily.

•

Yohan steps away from the conversation with the bartender, two pints of beer in his hands. They had met earlier that day. She went on about her love for whisky, while he listened patiently, taking in as much as he could about her.

Once he sits down, he and Doha share a quiet cheer. He sinks his lips into the dark-coloured beer topped with a thick band of foam.

"Do you know her?" Doha asks.

Yohan shakes his head. "Not really. Just ran into her once before."

"Where?"

"The Soju Club."

Doha makes a face, somewhere between a smile and a frown.

"She was talking to you."

"She is a bartender. She talks to everyone."

"Not for that long, and she started the conversation. Do you know her name?" Doha presses, grinning at Yohan's attempt to gloss over the topic.

"Her name is Seonhye," Yohan answers. "Park."

Doha looks surprised. "Seonhye Park? She is Korean?"

"It sounds like it."

"Where is she from?"

"She says Seoul."

"She came all the way here from Seoul for what?"

"She didn't say."

Doha raises his eyebrows and looks over to the bartender, now talking to another customer and cheerfully passing him a drink. "Aeminai is quite bold to be living on her own in a strange land," he mutters, taking a sip of beer.

"How do you know she is on her own?"

"A Korean girl, that young, working at a bar during night shifts, looking like that? It means she's here without anyone to hold her back. No mother, no father, no husband."

Yohan looks back and sees her laughing. Her small nose and her upturned eyes give him a slight impression of a cat. Her white tank top seems to almost shine in the dim light. He can see from her broad shoulders and toned arms that she is physically capable. Her makeup is light, yet her thin lips glow red, even as he looks from a distance.

"Happens more often than you think. Those Southerners leaving their own country. Supposed to be a paradise, yet their own people flee for a better place."

Yohan has seen pictures. Curtains of high-rises that spread endlessly on either side of the Han River. Dozen-lane city roads filled with cars. Men in T-shirts and women in short shorts. Neon signs of shops dangling messily from buildings. People freely going in and out of restaurants, bars, and clubs.

"Frankly, I don't believe in the concept of paradise," Doha says before taking another sip of his beer. "No place can be paradise. There's something wrong with every place. These people seek better lives by going elsewhere, and it's futile. They hop over to another place only to find that they've traded one kind of misery for another."

"What about us? We left home."

"We're different. We left home for a purpose. A mission for the republic. In a way we never left home."

As Doha talks, Yohan watches Seonhye serving drinks, leaning over the counter at times, looking at her patrons with alluring eyes. Then she glances over to his side and he looks away.

"Boston was pretty nice, though," Doha says, cradling his pint in his hands.

"Boston? In the United States?" Yohan looks at Doha, surprised.

"Yes. A long time ago."

"What for?"

"I was there, disguised as a Japanese translator. Boston because that's where Harvard is. That was the task. Go to the best school in the world and find out what they're doing right to improve the quality of our people's education."

Doha clasps his fingers into a ball, looking at Yohan with a smirk. Usually, it is a sign that he is about to say something he feels is profound. "But the mission was meaningless to begin with. The success of their education system was not about the system itself. These Americans, they believe in a self-driven future interrupted by no one, not by the government, not even by family. The desire to be their best selves by their own accord pushes them. That is the main fuel for their success."

"So then, what did you report back?"

"I wrote that their excellent medicine and law degree programs were of great value, providing their society with high-quality health and legal services. But of course, it was all nonsense. Americans pursue higher education because they are motivated by capitalistic desires and the allure of being able to command more money and status. Pyongyang would have never accepted that antirevolutionary bourgeois bullshit." Doha catches Yohan with a sly glance and laughs, his shoulders skipping a bit.

"But they were happy with that report. Not that they did anything with it. Nothing changed. It's usually how it is. It wasn't all fruitless, though, that trip," he says. "I enjoyed the city. Boston is lovely."

"What about here? Oxford?"

"This is a lovely place, too, but it's not quite the same."

Yohan thinks for a bit. He has learned that Americans are invaders. They are imperialists who spread their poison throughout the world under the guise of development and prosperity. His mission in life is to free the world, especially the South, of this American plague. At least this is what he learned in school back home. In real life, Yohan knows nothing about the Americans. In Oxford he would pass many of them dressed in their tourist garb. They tended to look naive, boisterous, but most of all harmless, hardly the portrait of vicious conquerors.

"Americans don't know modesty," Doha says. "They crave extremes and mask it under the veil of freedom. They work all waking hours to collect more money than they could ever spend. They shove more food down their throats despite it slowly killing them. Their race for more borders on insanity. But if you want, you can go and join that race. They have a word for that. It's called the American dream. I think it's a wonderful concept. Like everyone is living the same self-centred delusion."

Doha glides his fingertips along the rim of his glass, now empty. Then he scoops a small bit of foam from the edge and rubs it between his index finger and his thumb. "Try to capture that in a report."

He seems to be in a reverie. Yohan wonders just how many stories like this Doha has. Before coming to Europe, he was always flying in and out, so much so that when Yohan was young, he thought Doha lived in the skies.

"Well, in any case, you've had your first taste of them today," Doha says.

"Taste of what? The Americans?"

"This pub is an American cover. The girl you spoke to, Seonhye, she's American."

Yohan throws a confused glance at the bartender. "What are we doing here, then?"

"Observing, taking stock of it all. Not particularly a threat in my opinion, but it's still good to know who's who and what's here. When your enemies are close, you get closer. So close that you are literally staring back at them with your noses rubbing against each other."

"How so?"

"Because the other cannot make a move without risking something, and what's more, a third party cannot easily weasel their way in. As far as I know, this is the safest place we can be tonight."

"Right." Yohan nods and looks around. He spots Seonhye again. She is also looking around and then finds him. She waves at him, and he waves back.

"What do you think she wants from me?" Yohan asks, his arms crossed with his hands tucked into his armpits.

"Information, whatever it is."

"So she'll listen to anything I say?" Yohan muses.

"Precisely."

"And she'll keep talking, so she can keep me talking. And we can continue on like that as long as I never say who I really am?"

"That's right."

Yohan turns his head and watches Seonhye as she serves a series of shots to a trio of suit-clad workmates.

"I think I've finally found someone of my own age to talk to."

The Southerner

In the kitchen Jihoon checks that he has all the supplies he needs until the end of the week. His eyes go back and forth between the list written on his notepad and the ingredients in the fridge. Gochujang, doenjang, bean sprouts, zucchini, ham, pork belly, as well as the marinated pork and beef he prepared last night. The list goes on until he has flipped through three pages of inventory checks.

Someone unlocks the back door and opens it. "It's me," Deoksu calls out, his long black hair draped beneath his cap like a curtain around his neck and over his backpack.

"I'm in the kitchen," Jihoon says without lifting his eyes from the notepad. He checks the time and sees that Deoksu has come early, just like he asked. It's gimjang day, and they will make a batch of kimchi that will last for the entire month.

Deoksu joins Jihoon, wrapping an apron around his waist. He then tucks his hair into a bun with an elastic. "The cabbages have been salted, yeah?" he asks.

"Yes."

"Great, I'll start making the sauce."

Deoksu grabs a sack of gochugaru and starts pouring it into a large plastic bowl. He always seems to have a perfect sense of just how much he should use. It is the one thing that Jihoon was never able to learn from his mother — how to measure by memory.

"Thanks for coming in early. I really appreciate it."

Deoksu arrived after a week full of interviews with potential employees. One after the other, Jihoon found the candidates lacking. There would be someone who was perfect as a server but had zero merit in the kitchen. Another would be an excellent cook but could not hold four glasses on a tray properly. But

Deoksu seemed to be tailored for the position. He had prior experience as a cook and server in a Korean restaurant. He knew all the dishes and even suggested a few menu items that he could make, such as tteokbokki and suyuk. After listing everything he could do, he reached into his backpack and took out a small case of kimchi that he had made. It was perfect — not too ripe, not too sour. Not as good as Eomma's, but still perfect in its own way. Jihoon hired Deoksu on the spot.

Once the sauce for the kimchi is ready, Deoksu takes the cabbages one by one and spreads the sauce thoroughly, rubbing it between the leaves, all the way down to the stem. They'll be a bit too fresh to serve this week, but in two weeks they'll be perfect.

Jihoon notices that it is light outside. A few people are starting to walk past the restaurant, either on their way to work or school. He grabs two packs of instant ramen from a box stored in the corner of the kitchen. Ramen was the first thing he learned how to prepare when he was a child. His mother would often be working, and the one thing that was easy enough to make was a pack of ramen. He puts a pot of water on the stove and gathers various ingredients to put in the soup. Over the years he tinkered with the recipe, constantly trying to perfect it. Once the water boils, he puts in the soup powder, some old kimchi brine, sesame powder, minced garlic, sliced shiitake mushrooms, pork belly, and frozen clam meat. He inserts the uncooked noodles but takes them out before they are completely cooked. After adding a cup of whisked egg, he pours the soup equally into two bowls. Only then does he gently place the half-cooked noodles into each bowl. He sprinkles diced green onion and, as a finishing touch, adds a slice of cheese, which starts melting into the noodles right away. One bowl goes to Deoksu and the other is for himself. They share the meal on the kitchen island. Deoksu almost inhales the noodles and lets out a satisfying groan. "I don't get it. It's just different when you do it," he says.

"How different?" Jihoon asks.

"It's just better."

They laugh for a moment and continue to eat. It is peaceful, just the two of them slurping away at their noodles. It is possibly the only time of the day when they will get to share a meal without a customer asking for something. It is Jihoon's favourite time of the day.

•

At ten in the evening, when he has finished his second mock exam, Jihoon packs up. He looks around and sees the classroom still full of students at their desks. Jihoon has to leave now.

Instead of walking home, he walks in the opposite direction for thirty minutes, to his mother's restaurant. Jihoon slides the metal door open and sees his mother sweeping the floor. She stands and looks at him as he sheds his backpack and jacket and rolls up his sleeves. On the stove is a batch of anchovy broth stewing for the next day.

"What are you doing here?"

"I'm here to help."

"I don't need your help. You can study, that's how you can help."

Even as she is scolding him, he goes to the back and starts washing the dishes, as he always does. She stands next to him and tells him to sort out the dried anchovies instead, rolling her sleeves up. Jihoon grabs a pair of red rubber gloves and hands them to his mother.

"I don't need those," she says. "Give me the dishes."

"C'mon, Eomma. You'll ruin your hands if you don't."

"Aicham!" She snatches the gloves from Jihoon and hastily shoves her hands in.

"You shouldn't come in the evenings anymore."

"Why not?"

"You need to study."

"I'm fine. I'll be fine."

"It won't be fine if you botch your Suneung."

Jihoon has nothing to say to this. He knows his mother's concerns for his upcoming exam, and he is doing everything he can for it. After they are done with the dishes, Jihoon finishes with prep for tomorrow while his mother counts the day's money. He smells and tastes the anchovy broth, confirms that it is ready. He puts the lid back on the pot and leaves it to cool down so it can be stored in the fridge for later. His mother is putting the cash into her bag and closes the register. She pauses, looks at Jihoon, and takes out a few notes of ten thousand won for him.

They exit the restaurant, and she puts a padlock on the door. She holds Jihoon's arm, and they walk down the dimly lit street together. He notices how frail her grip is and how slow he must walk to keep pace with her. He cannot believe that she walks home on her own almost every night. When they finally reach their basement dwelling, he rolls out two sets of bedding on the floor. She sits and he massages her shoulder, unprompted. She tells him that it is okay, but she does not refuse after Jihoon starts to press on her muscles.

"Is this better?" he asks as he pushes his thumb into a particularly tense knot.

"Yes, yes. Feels a bit too much. Softer, please."

When his mother falls asleep, exhausted from the day, Jihoon turns on a small flashlight in the corner of the one room they share and goes over the answers of his earlier mock exams. He pulls a blanket over himself so as not to wake her since she will be up at five in the morning. Finding that his answers are mostly correct, he smiles in relief. He quietly goes to the closet and opens it. Underneath his socks is a small bank account book. He brings it under the blanket and examines it. This month he did extra shifts at the convenience store near the school. His mother does not know about it, but as long as he keeps his exam scores up, he suspects it will not be a problem.

By Suneung he will have enough. He will be able to buy two plane tickets and reserve seven nights of accommodation. They'll spend half of the trip in London, then the other half in Paris. He reminds himself to drop by the bank to deposit the notes that his mother gave him. He turns off the flashlight and crawls in the dark to his bedding, next to his mother. When he lies down, he turns to face where his mother is and watches her in peaceful sleep until his eyes close as well from the weight of the day.

The American

They carry the body up a flight of stairs, open the door to their living quarters, and drop Doha on the dining table. Out of breath, Yunah places her hand on her hip and looks down at the legendary North Korean spymaster, whose decades-long career has come to an end. Blood is pooling under him and dripping off the edge of the table. She and Thomas look at Doha Kim's corpse for a while, both unable to come up with any words.

"What now?" Yunah finally asks.

"I guess I'll contact headquarters. Then we start closing it all off."

Yunah sighs. "What the fuck was the point of all this?"

"What are you so upset about? We got him," Thomas says, pointing at Doha.

"We got nothing; we did nothing. We barely figured out anything. Their whole network just crumbled on their own. We can't end it like this. We have to find him."

"Don't bring up Junichi Nakamura again. We're not going after that guy."

"Why not?"

"Listen, just think about it. They just killed Doha Kim. Who do you think they're going after next?"

"All the more reason why we should bring him in."

"Okay, let's say we do. Do you think we have the resources to defend him? We have no idea what the other side is capable of. They can blow this entire block up for all we know. We have one pistol that we share."

"Thomas, there is someone out there who can help us to salvage all of this. He can tell us what's happening. He can give us the full picture. I think that's worth the risk. Besides, we can call for backup."

"Yunah, please. I'm not going to argue. The body is enough. We can at least write up that his spy cell is now done. That there is no more Doha Kim. What you're suggesting is going off the rails."

"Fine, whatever." Yunah has had enough. She knows she won't get through to Thomas. She always knew that he lacked the kind of hunger that she always had, to go further than what was required. Thomas was the strict rule-follower. He was quicker to write up a report than to actually spring into action.

"Hey," he calls out. "Gun."

Of course, the one gun. She stomps her way to the safe box on top of the file cabinet, unholsters her pistol, and shoves it in. "Happy?"

Thomas holds up a thumb. Yunah shakes her head at him.

She goes downstairs. In the empty pub, she takes a bottle of Lagavulin off the wall and sits at a table in the corner. She pops the top open and takes a swig. Her phone vibrates and she sees it's her father. Usually, she ignores these calls, but she picks up this time. It must be late there, nearly midnight. Her parents have been night owls for long.

"Yunah-ya! How are you doing over there?" he asks in Korean.

"I'm okay," she says in English.

"They say it's cold in England. Is it cold?"

"It's not. It's not an issue."

"Are you coming for Seollal?"

"Depends on work."

"You said that last year."

She can hear her mother's *tsk* in the background. "Give me the phone," her mother says.

"Hi, Eomma."

"Why don't you ask for a vacation?"

"I can't."

"Tell them it's important. Koreans have to get together for Seollal."

"I'm sorry, but it's just not a good time right now. I'll come when I can."

"She has work. It's important work. Government work. Don't bother her," her father says — now in the background — disregarding her mother's protests.

"Family is also very important. If the government doesn't see that, then why do we bother paying our taxes?" her mother says. Yunah hears the faint sound of her mother slapping her father, presumably on the shoulder or the back. Those are the usual spots.

"Aicham, stop with your nonsense. Ignore your mother. Work is more important."

Her father is easier to handle. There is clarity with his wishes. She just needs to be excellent. Fortunately, her father's wishes align well with her own goals. Her mother is another story.

"Yeobo, please, I'm talking. You know, if you come to Seollal, you can come to church with us. So many people want to see you."

Church occupies a very distinct but thankfully distant part of her memory as an absolutely insufferable place. As soon as Yunah entered university and was able to get away from her family, she vowed to never step foot in a church again, especially if it were a Korean church.

"Who wants to see me?"

"Many people. Don't you like people from church? You have so many friends there."

"They're not my friends anymore," she says.

"You still know people. Do you remember Mrs. Bong's son? He's now a managing director at a — Yeobo, what was it?"

"An investment bank," her father says.

"That's right, investment bank. Big investment bank."

Usually when these conversations arise, Yunah simply cuts them off by abruptly saying that she has to go. This time, though, her curiosity encourages her to entertain them a bit longer. "What's his name?"

"Jimmy, I think. Jimmy Bong."

"Oh yeah, Jimmy Bong."

"Yes! You remember Jimmy Bong. He's a nice boy, right?"

On paper Jimmy Bong could be a catch. Decent looking, with money. Unfortunately, Jimmy is also a bratty manchild whose ego is paired with ironclad unawareness. She can hardly see how anyone is able to overlook his terrible conversational skills and his habit of talking on and on about his achievements. She used to wonder where his booming confidence came from, but whenever she saw his parents parade him around like he was a medal from the president, she knew whose fault it was.

"I already know Jimmy."

"Get to know him better, then."

"I don't want to get to know him better."

"You should give him a try."

"I'm not giving Jimmy a try, Eomma."

"You never listen."

"I never listen to what?"

"Never mind. Forget it. *Tsk.*"

Yunah sighs. Their conversations always end like this. Whether it is Jimmy Bong one week, Edmund Jeong another week, or Chris Park the next month. There is always someone new for her to meet.

"Whatever, I'll just go to bed now. Bye," her mother says and passes the phone to her father.

"Your eomma is mad now, but it won't last long," her father says.

"Yeah," she sighs.

"She's like a pot. She bubbles up, calms down later. You know how it goes."

She does know how it goes. The problem lies with her mother's relentlessness. She has never stopped reminding Yunah about how she needs to be the next person in a white dress, walking down the aisle, with a Korean man waiting at the altar.

"But do visit, Yunah. We want to see you."

"I'll try."

"Okay, talk to you soon," her father says in heavily accented English.

"Bye, Appa."

She shuts her phone and sighs in exhaustion, trying to tuck the conversation into a corner of her mind so she doesn't analyze every single thing her mother said. She didn't want to take the call because she knew she'd be in a foul mood at the end of it. Another quick swig from the Lagavulin burns her throat on its way down, but it does little to lighten her mood.

The botched mission in Oxford would mar her otherwise perfect record. Every time she goes into her old bedroom in her childhood home, during the odd visits she makes on holidays, she feels like it is a shrine to someone she doesn't know anymore. There are tae kwon do trophies resting on shelves, next to her medals from track and field, her diploma from Harvard, and photos with dignitaries from various exclusive events. There is even one with the Clintons, from when she was invited to the White House for winning a sustainability project competition. All this glory and winning. Her parents were adamant about one thing — whatever they did, they had to try three times harder than those born and raised in America. They were uninvited guests taking space in a country, so they had to prove themselves. This was why their bagel store always had a clean, well-stocked bathroom and why her father always smiled at his guests, even when an angry customer called him a "dirty Chink." When she moved to protest, her father held her back. "The man already paid me for his sandwich. So who's winning here, exactly?"

Winning while losing, he called it. So maybe this is the same. The operation is not a failure, but it's not a success either. None of it feels right.

As she drinks alone in the pub, she sees the air conditioner in the corner. It doesn't work, but it's a convenient spot to hide a camera in.

"Air-con," she utters, forgetting to not pronounce the *r*.

Cole, one of her handlers, thought it was essential she pose as a South Korean. According to him, a true South Korean would have an accent, and she was given a crash course in how to be Korean without being Korean. She remembers the pursed lips of the speech therapist from Idaho, who received her Ph.D. in Korean from the University of Edinburgh in the U.K.

"Ae-eo-cawn."

"Air-con."

"No, you see, you're pronouncing the *r*. Skip it. Just go *ae* and *eo*."

She feels stupid as she says it. "Ae-eo."

"Cawn."

"Con."

"No, it's not con. It's like, somewhere between con and cun. Like cunning."

Or cunt.

"Air-con," she says again after a swig of her whisky, forgetting to omit the *r* yet again. "Ssibal, ae-eo-con."

That one was from her dad. Ssibal to the guy who cut him off on the highway. Ssibal to the nick on his finger while chopping vegetables. Ssibal to the contractor who ruined a simple renovation job. Ssibal to the bank who wouldn't approve his loan. Ssibal to life when everything is going to shit.

"Ssibal Oxford," Yunah says.

CHAPTER 3

The Northerner

DOHA ALWAYS SAID THAT IN EVERY CITY, THERE IS A rhythm and that Yohan must be aware of this rhythm and flow with it when necessary. In London or Berlin, the city awakes and that rhythm starts abruptly. In Oxford it is a trickle.

Yohan is loitering in an alley behind a building, right across from the Magpie. He is listening on an earpiece connected to a device he had planted under the bar a long time ago. So far, it is as expected. The Americans have called it in and alerted headquarters. They're planning to clean the place up and close it all down. He can see the pub as he hears them talk. He can imagine the wooden beams under which Seonhye must be pacing while the man, known as Roland on paper, is talking to her about their immediate plans from behind the dark brown bar that stretches across half the pub's length.

It was Doha's idea to make the pub Junichi's go-to place. To make it look like he was being lured in by the bartender, Seonhye.

"Won't they think it's odd?"

"Maybe, but Americans are not used to their plans falling apart," Doha said to him. "And as long as things are going their way, they're not going to pay much attention."

Yohan knows this is the case because there have been times when Seonhye has tried to ask him questions. Yohan has never revealed much to her, except weaving the story of Junichi Nakamura and stretching that thread as far as he can. She chats him up every night and tries to get the conversation going until Yohan has to physically pry himself away from the bar and call it a day. She always talks as if she is an open book, giving him intimate details about what he assumes is her cover. Seonhye, as she says, is Korean. She is from Korea, born and raised there. However, she always avoids speaking the language, saying she is here to practise English rather than speak Korean. Her English is impeccable, so much so that she pronounces Seoul as "Soul" instead of "Saw-ool."

Roland mentions that they need to go to Doha's flat. Yohan thinks he has covered their tracks but remembers the hidden gun. He wonders whether he should try to recover it, but the Americans are fast. The two rush out of the pub's front door and get into a grey Volvo. He'll never get there in time. He gives up on the gun.

Once the car is out of sight, Yohan emerges and walks to the Magpie. The first floor of the two-storey building is the pub, and it is littered with concealed cameras, even in the bathrooms. There is one hidden at the centre of the clock on the wall. Another is inside the letter *o* on the label of a bottle of whisky. So far, he has counted thirteen hidden cameras. The second floor is where the Americans live and keep all their equipment. It is where the real work is done. There are two access points, one through the front door and another through the back door. Both entrances guarantee getting caught by cameras.

He looks around. There is no one on the streets right now. No cars are passing by. He swiftly climbs the building's facade and perches on a window ledge on the second floor. He tries the window and finds it is locked. He takes out a small pocket knife, fits it between the sash and the windowsill, and presses the knife down until the lock pops out of its place. He enters a room with two bunk beds and a small table with a digital alarm clock sitting on top. He steps into the living room, where he finds two chairs, a desk, and a filing cabinet with an open safe on top. He goes back to his pocket knife and pulls out a pin tool. Once he unlocks the cabinet, he goes through various documents that outline profiles of him and his mentor, Doha Kim. They also have information on all his colleagues strewn across Europe, all of them now dead.

There is a password-protected laptop. He tries the trick that Doha taught him, which is to reload the computer with safe mode. It works, but he finds nothing of interest. The email account has another layer of password protection, which will be trickier to get through. There is a small trash can beside a fax machine in the corner of the living room. He looks inside and sees pieces of ripped paper. He pours the contents onto the floor and starts reassembling the pieces. He is able to form two pages outlining a plan to retrieve Junichi Nakamura by sending in two new agents. He sees their photos. One is a woman with light hair and the other is a heavily bearded man. He remembers their faces, names, and profiles. Afterward, he jumbles up the pieces and puts them back in the trash can.

Finally, he checks the dining room and comes across Doha's body. He is startled to see him like this, laid out on the table as if he is a trophy from a hunt. Yohan approaches. His hand hovers over where Doha was stabbed. The knife went deep into his stomach, cutting the aorta in his abdominals. He was barely conscious when Yohan got to him and bled to death only minutes after being attacked.

Yohan looks down at the man who gave him everything. The closest he's ever had to a father. He ponders the tightening of his chest and wonders if this is real sorrow. He holds Doha's hand, now cold and dry. He remembers seeing children holding hands with their parents, realizing that he has never held anyone's hand like that before. He wishes Doha would sit up and tell him it was all an elaborate test, but he doesn't. Doha is truly gone, and he is on his own.

"Goodbye, seonsaeng-nim," he says as he lets go of the hand.

He checks whether the street is still empty, then quickly makes his exit through the window.

•

Three days after Doha confirms with Pyongyang that the Brussels operative has gone missing, they locate him in Norway. Yohan takes a morning flight to Bergen. After taking a cab to the city centre, he walks to the small fourth-floor lodging he had rented, from which he can see directly into the window of his target's apartment.

Over the course of a week, he maps out his target's patterns. He has grown a light beard since Yohan last saw him. He steps out of his apartment every day in the mid-afternoon and gets back around dinnertime, anywhere between 1800 to 1900 hours. He also jogs regularly in the mornings. Usually, the same route down the hill, through the city centre to the docks, and then back up.

Yohan initiates his plan on the eighth day. He watches the target, clad in a black jacket and jeans, stroll out the building's front entrance. Yohan waits for an hour and then walks across the street, entering the target's building. He climbs a narrow set of stairs past the front door. On the third flight of stairs, he turns to the target's door, picks the lock, and opens it. Inside, he inches forward, looking out for wires. He is greeted by a modest dwelling. A single bed, a table, a chair, and a stool by the fridge. It is a mirror image of the space that he is temporarily occupying.

Yohan goes to the window, pulls back the curtains, and looks outside. The day is cloudy, and few people are in the streets. Beyond, he sees a mountain rising above the city. By his calculations, the man will arrive in approximately two hours. He drags the chair a bit so that he will be facing the door directly when the target enters the flat.

When the man returns after exactly two hours, he holds a bag of groceries in his arms. He sees Yohan sitting on the chair. Yohan nods at him, and he nods back, calm as a host finding a guest who has arrived early.

"Dongmu, you're finally here," the target says, setting the groceries on the counter and lowering himself onto the stool. The Hamkyeongdo accent is heavy in his Korean.

Yohan does not answer. His protocol is clear on these missions — do not engage, simply execute.

"I saw you, dongmu. I was wondering when you'd come over. Your unit is small, isn't it? I think the apartment I used to have with my omani back home was much larger."

The man, leaning his arm on his knee, smirks momentarily and then looks at the floor. It makes Yohan uneasy, and he wonders if there is something under the floorboard. It's the one place he didn't look when he was sweeping the apartment for weapons.

The man stands up and moves toward the kettle on the stove. "Would you like some tea?"

Yohan does not respond. The man takes his silence as agreement and simply carries on, putting two bags of black tea into two mugs — one red and one grey with a small triangular piece chipped away on the edge, leaving a short trail of forking cracks beneath. The gas stove heats up, the blue flames flaring up after a quiet *tick-tick-tick* and a *whip*. The green kettle's bottom is blackened; the fire licks at it hungrily, familiarly.

"There is no hurry," the man says. "I'm not going to run from this."

Yohan hears thumps from above; someone is stomping around upstairs. He can clearly make out a woman talking in the unit next to them. She sounds angry, like she is accusing someone.

"It's a bit noisy here. I thought it'd be nice and quiet in Norway. Turns out people are people everywhere."

Yohan leans back and, with steady eyes, observes the man.

"I suppose this is as expected," the man says, looking out the window. "I don't know what I wanted to find. I suppose that's why I haven't left, though I should've."

The kettle whistles. Yohan readies himself, expecting the other man to hurl boiling water at him while he makes a break for it. But he does not. Instead, he serves tea in slow, relaxed movements.

"How is he doing? Our Commander Doha," he asks Yohan, his hands wrapped around his mug.

Yohan does not answer but instead glances around the room, vigilant for an unseen threat or surprise.

"Please, dongmu. Do spare your comrade some companionship in his last moments. Have some tea. It was very expensive. Here, everything is."

Yohan sniffs first, then presses the edge of the cup to his lips. Once he confirms that it does not taste off, he takes a fuller sip.

"Is it good?" The target grins expectantly.

Yohan tips his head a bit, not to give an answer but to simply respond.

"Ah, I was hoping for more of a reaction. I suppose money doesn't exactly buy better tea. Capitalist lies and whatnot." He shakes his head, takes a sip from his cup, and then puts the mug down on the small table next to him and leans in with his hands pressed together. "Tea from home was much better. All these different tastes, all these different choices, yet nothing compares to the little we had. I miss it dearly. Do you not miss home?" he asks Yohan.

After a pause the man chuckles. "Right, maybe not as much as I do. I have my omani back home, you see. When they sent us out here, they sent us out here with nothing. Not even a picture." The man drifts off for a while, setting his gaze on a place beyond the room. "Do you know what that's like? To forget your own omani's face? It started with not remembering what her ears looked like. Soon after, parts of her face started disappearing from my memory. It spread to her mouth. I forgot how her lips formed when she would speak. How her smile curled up to her cheeks. She had this endless smile for me. The way her face would fold in a thousand different places. And before I realized what was happening, I lost her nose one day. And then her cheeks. And then her eyes. Her face became a blank canvas. Like those egg ghosts you heard from folk tales, yeah? Their faces just erased, a flat, smooth surface with nothing on them."

The comrade rubs his eyes, sighing, the story taking a toll on him. "Then I saw her one night. I dreamed of her. She was wearing this white jeogori and chima. She was telling me that she was waiting for me. I asked her where she was waiting and she wouldn't say. Why would she come to me then? After all that time? I had to think something was wrong."

With a quick glance, Yohan checks his watch. He hopes he won't have to cut the comrade short. It is the last courtesy he wants to show him.

"So I asked the commander. I asked him if he could send her a message for me and he told me he couldn't. I asked whether she was living in an apartment in Kaesong like he told me. He refused to answer and said that it was classified. Why would that be classified? I just wanted to know that she was okay, that she was provided for like the Dear Leader promised. That was all I wanted to know. But the commander told me I didn't need to know anything. Only to accept what I've been told. Because his word was the word of the Leader. But I knew that something was off because the dreams never stopped. She kept appearing, telling me that she was sorry. I kept asking her why she was sorry, but she simply kept crying. I knew something had happened to her. They said my omani would be taken care of, yet she could be in the camps for all I know."

Yohan recognizes a familiar look in the comrade's face. It is the face of silent desperation that he has seen only in other children at the orphanage. The kind that creeps over when the situation is life or death, yet there is nothing that can be done. When hunger can't be helped because there simply is no food or when pain from wounds can't be relieved because no one cares for you.

The man flashes Yohan a bitter grin. "In a way, you are the fortunate one, my dongmu. You have nothing you're tethered to. You're a floater. You know nothing about what it means to have someone who depends on you, who is connected to you. You've never been someone to anyone."

Yohan holds his silence. His grip on his cup tightens slightly. He says nothing back because there is no need to respond. Doha instructed him to not say anything and simply carry out the task.

"You must see it. We are all dead already. The moment we stepped on this foreign soil to do our duty, we all became empty husks. I really thought this would be the best for all of us. I thought I was doing something for my omani back home. So I left with hope in my heart. But all I want now is to taste my omani's stew."

The man sighs, and it looks as if he has finally made a decision he has put off for a long time. He finishes his tea in one gulp and puts his mug in the sink. "Well, how will we do this?"

"A pill."

"Which one?"

Yohan takes a small black box from his coat and opens it, revealing a white pill with a red stripe.

"Ah, this one. At least Commander Doha shows me mercy. What will they say about me?" he asks.

Yohan begins to recite what the commander prepared. "You were on a mission to intercept a Russian politician's meeting with the Norwegians, but a Namjoseon spy discovered you. Your pursuers got close. They almost had you. As they were ramming down the door, you realized there was no way out, so you committed suicide and went down without spilling a word to the republic's enemies."

He nods with each beat of the story, listening carefully to Yohan's words. "Good," he says. "Not that it matters."

The comrade plucks the pill from its container and stares at it. He drags it around his palm with his index finger, lifts his head, and grins. Yohan has never seen this kind of serenity in a man about to die. He has always had to do it either by force or without the target's knowledge. Yohan points his chin to the pill, telling the comrade to get on with it.

"I hope you find something for yourself in the end, dongmu." He pops it quickly in his mouth, swallowing once. He walks over to the bed, lies down, and closes his eyes. There is no struggle nor the slightest utterance of pain on his lips. He simply falls asleep. After five minutes Yohan gets up and leans his head toward the man's chest. There is no heartbeat.

Yohan collects the comrade's gear, hidden in the cupboards behind a false panel, a standard set-up according to Doha's training manual for his operatives. There he also finds the comrade's money and identification. He takes all but one of the passports and leaves it on the table for whoever discovers the body.

The Southerner

Jihoon likes to be alone. He likes to spend nights by himself, slowly drinking and reading until sleep takes him and he turns in for the day. It is a routine that he has never quite broken since he arrived in Oxford and opened his restaurant.

When his mother used to run her restaurant back in Seoul, people called her by her name and she remembered everyone who came in. She knew the lives of her regulars from the nearby factory, who would come in to eat lunch and have drinks in the evening. They would loudly declare their arrival and find their usual waiting for them because she already knew what they would want.

Jihoon tried to do the same with his restaurant, but he has found getting people to remember his name difficult. And he also can't seem to remember his customers either. He used to wonder how his mother managed to maintain such intimacy with her customers. Now he just keeps it simple. He greets with a "hello," gives menus, takes orders, brings out the food, and accepts payment at the end. None of this has to involve speaking. He just smiles and bobs his head in acknowledgement, and that is enough for most interactions.

Then there are the Koreans, with whom he allows himself to be more spontaneous, partly because of the language but also because of how they can talk about Korea without much effort. There are usually two kinds — tourists and students. With tourists it's a simple matter. They talk about home and how they miss home in different ways. For them it's an inconvenience, like how they can't find a public toilet in Oxford compared to Seoul. Or how they find the subway stations in London cramped, hot, and ugly.

For Jihoon it's a longing. It's about wanting to look back to the good moments of his past. Rather than missing the small things, it's about the feelings that cannot be replicated. This is why, perhaps, he finds the conversations with students more relatable. They have a similar sense of longing. They are here for years and rarely go back because of money issues. A plane ticket home is expensive, and only the few truly wealthy students can afford such luxury often. They talk about wanting to see their parents. They talk about meals at home and how they feel like they stand out in a crowd. But even they eventually go home. Once they return, there will be someone waiting for them at the airport. For Jihoon the Soju Club is all he has. He looks at the empty restaurant. He thinks briefly about closing early today.

"Hyung, smoke?" Deoksu asks as he twirls the toothpick in his mouth after finishing the ramen.

Without answering, Jihoon pulls out the pack from his pocket, takes two, and hands Deoksu one. They step outside, stand on the curb, and light their cigarettes.

They are now in the in-between hours, when the city's morning rush turns into a trickle, as most people have reached their destinations, whether it's a classroom or an office. Not that it matters to Jihoon. Business at the Soju Club doesn't start until lunchtime. The British aren't interested in hot stew or bowls of rice for breakfast, which is peculiar to Jihoon considering that their version of breakfast is even heavier than a hangover stew.

"Hyung-nim, I'm planning to leave," Deoksu says.

Jihoon briefly chokes on his smoke and coughs. "Leave? To where?"

"Back home."

"Home? So back to Seoul?"

"No, Pohang."

"You said you were from Seoul."

"Well, I came here from Seoul, yeah. But I was born in Pohang. I moved to Seoul when I was in elementary school."

"So you still kind of grew up in Pohang?"

"Sort of. I don't remember much. Had a grandmother there. She lived in this really tiny apartment, and whenever we went down there, we would all have to sleep in one room. It was literally just that — one room, a kitchen, and a toilet. I remember hating it because back in Seoul I had my own room."

Deoksu flicks the ash from his cigarette. "I mean, I still liked my grandmother. I'd ask why she couldn't live with us in Seoul, and they said it was because she was too old to travel. Thing is, I didn't know that she was dying at the time, because of *this*," he says, looking at the cigarette in his hand.

"Ah," Jihoon utters. "But why Pohang instead of Seoul?"

"Hyung-nim, have you seen the house prices?"

"Well, no, I haven't gone back in a while."

"Are you thinking of going back any time soon?"

"I'm not going back," Jihoon says with a shake of his head.

"Like never? You're never going to go back?"

"Never."

"I'm sure you will. All Koreans, no matter how far we go, no matter how much we forget or ignore it, we all miss home. That's why we're so happy to see one another abroad."

Jihoon wonders whether he misses home or if it's something else entirely that he is feeling. Either that or he doesn't care.

"We're like salmon. Nobody tells us to swim upstream toward the homeland, but we always do."

"Not everyone's like that."

"I mean, if you're not, then you're not Korean. Simple as that. Like those second-generation kids who don't speak a lick of the language. They're not Korean. They're some other morons, ssibal."

Deoksu frowns and forcefully spits onto the pavement before taking a draw on his cigarette again. "I mean, how are you even a Korean when you don't speak the language? You might as well be one of those Jap collaborators from colonial times. These people living abroad, they're not Koreans and fuck 'em if they think they are. They're only Korean when it's low stakes. Like when we're in the World Cup or it's the Olympics. If war breaks out tomorrow with the North, you think those Koreans will go back home to help us fight? You think those Koreans will donate a dime? No. It's people like me, people like us."

Deoksu points to himself and then to Jihoon. It's like a lid has popped off a boiling pot. He continues without skipping a beat. "I got a feeling that you're a Korean. A real one. Someone who cares about the motherland. And that's a feeling that only real Koreans know."

"Right" is all that Jihoon can manage to say. "So you're leaving."

"Yeah. I came here wanting to see Europe. I saw enough of it. Now it's time to go back." He smiles at Jihoon like a delinquent would to a police officer to defuse a situation. "Thanks for taking care of me. Who would have helped me out here but you? Hiring a guy who speaks no English."

"No, you helped me much more."

"Aigo cham, hyung-nim-ah, why are you like this? Your shoulders are sagging. Don't worry, you'll find someone great to replace me."

Jihoon never thought about how he would feel if he lost Deoksu. He kept his concerns short sighted, whether it was about grocery deliveries or meeting his rent. Planning for the future or even contingencies that seemed distant were never on his mind. But he feels it now. It is as if a lump has formed inside his chest and is pressing against his heart. Jihoon's mother used to say that everyone in the restaurant, whether a guest or a server, is family, partaking in a shared ritual day in and day out. Though Jihoon does not feel close to Deoksu, he understands what his mother meant. Deoksu can be relied on, but more importantly, he reminds Jihoon that he exists. No matter how much Jihoon tries to be invisible in this place and hide behind his immigrant self, Deoksu always tries to push past the mask.

"I'll tell you what: I'll get a place in Pohang and you'll always be welcome. Hell, just come live with me. Let's go get some gopchang, daechang, kkeopdaegi, you know, all of that good stuff that we can't get here."

"And some soju."

"Of course, soju."

Jihoon takes his last draw on the cigarette, which is now burning only a hair's width away from his fingertips. He feels its warmth and closes his eyes, thinking of Korea's stuffy summer air, the narrow streets filled with restaurants and bars, and a friend to roam through the city with. He thinks about taking up Deoksu's invitation to Pohang.

He is not ready for it. Not yet.

•

His exam is only a week away. These are the most crucial days. Every minute counts and he must spend all his time absorbing one more piece of knowledge. This is why he has his notes while watching the cash register at the convenience store. The manager does not mind that he reads his notes during the shift. He understands that Jihoon is a high school student. Not only that, but he is in his third year, the season of Suneung.

The door rings and Jihoon quickly calls out "Welcome." He looks up and, to his surprise, finds his mother right in front of him. "Eomma," he says, almost to himself.

His mother looks at him with an expression Jihoon has never seen before. There is an absolute stillness on her face. Jihoon wants her to say something, scold him, even start slapping him over his head. Anything would do. Choked by the silence, Jihoon opens his mouth.

"Eomma, I can explain."

But his mother is already leaving. He goes after her and steps out the door. Jihoon faces a choice. Abandon his post and follow his mother or wait until the shift is over. His eyes dart between the shop and the back of his mother as she walks farther away. He looks up at the sky, dark and cloudy, and then closes his eyes for a few seconds. Once he opens his eyes, his mother is out of sight. He goes back into the store.

When he is released from his shift, he runs home and finds his mother reading in the corner, her back turned to the door. He carefully enters, putting his bag down without making noise. He wants to talk to her, tell her that he has a plan for everything. If she asks about the exam, he will tell her that he has it under control. He pulls his books out and dares not look at his mother.

"Are you hungry?" she asks, startling him.

For a moment, Jihoon freezes, not knowing how to respond to this. "I'm okay."

"Do they feed you?"

"Who?"

"The convenience store."

"The manager gives me the triangle gimbaps that are close to expiring."

"Good."

Then she closes the book she was reading, pulls out bedding from the closet, and spreads it out for sleep. Jihoon looks over and sees that his mother was reading through the ledger for the restaurant.

"Eomma."

"What?"

"I'm sorry."

"Why are you sorry?"

"I should've told you. I'm sorry."

A pause. Then she pulls the blanket over her shoulder.

In the morning, like every other day, she has left a breakfast on the small table for him. When he opens the umbrella-shaped covering, he finds miyeok guk. Its rich smell awakens him, and he dips a spoonful of rice underneath the soup before taking a bite. The beef is cooked to just the perfect degree of tenderness.

Then he sees a piece of paper tucked between the bowl of miyeok guk and the small plate of kimchi. It says, "Happy Birthday, Son." He has forgotten his own birthday. He is now eighteen.

The American

The North Koreans' flat is a narrow place near Wellington Square. There's not much inside. The walls are bare, though in some places, Yunah can see the faint rectangular shapes left by picture frames that had been there for a long time. According to property purchase data, the house was bought at almost double the market price.

"What are we looking for, exactly?"

She turns to Thomas, who crosses his arms and leans against the closed door. "We're not looking for anything."

"But you said that we had new orders. To sweep the place."

"There are new orders. I've been ordered to keep you here no matter what."

Yunah stands in silence for a few seconds, thinking about what was just said. "When did that come down?"

"Right after we got his body." Thomas lifts his shirt and reveals the waistband holster holding the one pistol they share.

"Wow, so that's how it is."

"Yeah, that's how it is."

Yunah has become used to the stern, apathetic look that Thomas gives, but this time, she feels genuine contempt for it. It's his tone that she detests, like his hands are tied and there's nothing he can do about it.

She walks into the living room and drops down on the sofa. She looks around and sees a TV, another beaten couch, a wooden coffee table, and a whisky cabinet filled with bottles. She sees that there's a bottle of Glenmorangie 25, unopened. She seizes it by the neck and takes a crystal tumbler from the bottom shelf.

"What are you doing?" Thomas asks as he follows her into the living room.

"It's not like Doha Kim is going to drink this. I might as well. There's nothing else to do here."

Thomas sighs and also grabs a tumbler.

"Shouldn't you stay sober while watching your prisoner?" Yunah says with a scoff.

"Like I said, I'm just doing what I was told. You're not my prisoner. I'm waiting too. I have nothing else to do either."

"Whatever."

She pours a finger's worth for him first and then for herself. Thomas raises the glass and, after a bit of hesitation, she taps his glass with her own.

"They're looking to bring him in," Thomas says after the first sip. "Just to let you know."

"Junichi?"

"Yeah."

"Who's doing it?"

"Someone is coming in from London, another is flying in from Berlin."

"I should be there. I know him the best."

"That's the problem. They think you're too biased."

"Too biased? For what?"

"They think you're emotionally invested. That you can't be trusted to make a sound judgment."

"Based on what?"

"My report."

"Your report? Your report about me?" She points to herself.

"Yes, I've been writing reports regarding the mission. They said that you being Korean was a risk factor. That there was a possibility that you would empathize with the target, so I was to keep an eye out for that."

"Funny, I remember them saying that me being Korean was an asset."

"They said that too. It's not always clear-cut, is it?"

"For you it is, I guess. You're apparently neither a risk factor nor an asset."

"Lucky me," Thomas says.

She takes another sip, then shakes her head. "Why are you even here, Tommy? Why did you take this? Why not sit behind a desk if you're not going to even try?"

"We're here to do a mission. It's about doing what we were assigned to do. Look at what you're doing. You might have actually had a shot at Junichi Nakamura if you hadn't talked to him so often."

She stands up and leans in until her nose is almost touching his. "So this is my fault. Except you're the one who's writing reports on me behind my back." She finishes the rest of the glass and then puts the tumbler down on the coffee table.

"Like I said, I had my orders."

"Yeah, fuck you too."

Yunah steps over Thomas's legs and he grabs her arm.

"Where are you going?"

"Can I take a piss?"

Thomas lets her go and stands up to follow. She silently scowls back at him. She walks into the hallway and enters the bathroom, turns on the light, and closes the door as Thomas watches her. The bathroom is cramped. A shower, a sink, and a toilet all huddled together. She sits on the toilet lid and stares at the tiled wall in front of her, trying to decide what to do. She suddenly notices a tile that is ever so slightly out of alignment with the other tiles. She reaches for it, at first gliding her index finger along the shape of the tile. It moves a bit, so she picks at the edges. A gap forms. With both hands, she scrapes at the tile and, eventually, it comes up. She sets the tile down and sees a makeshift nook in the drywall. She finds something glistening inside. She slips her hand in, and when she is certain about what the object is, she slowly drags out a black pistol.

It is a Glock 42. She unloads the magazine and sees that it is full. There are no spare clips inside the hole in the wall nor is there any space for them. This is a backup gun, hidden from sight and reserved for the worst. Yunah stands up, her grip tightening around the gun. The fact that she has even a tiny bit of leverage feels good. She tucks the gun behind her back and pulls her top over to conceal it. She puts the missing tile back into place.

When she opens the bathroom door, she sees Thomas with his finger at his lips, gesturing to the front door with his head. There's a knock. He unholsters his gun and checks it. Yunah stays behind the bathroom door, only her head peeking out. When Thomas looks out the living room window to see if there is anyone outside, the front door bursts open and a man with a motorcycle helmet enters. He raises a silenced pistol quicker than Thomas can draw his own and, with a loud *pop*, fires a round into Thomas, who falls to the ground with a thud. The man in the helmet kicks away Thomas's pistol.

Yunah emerges from behind the bathroom door and fires two rounds. The man in the helmet quickly rolls out of the way, out of her sight. With her gun alert at her shoulders, Yunah slowly approaches the living room. She controls her breathing, keeping her iron sight steady while focused on the corner. Something rolls by her feet, so she looks down. It's a flash-bang.

She whips her head away, collapsing onto the floor as she shuts her eyes and covers her ears with her hands. Nothing happens. She glances at the stun grenade and sees that the pin is still in. A ruse. She feels a tug on her pistol and clutches her weapon close to her chest while positioning her legs above her torso to defend herself. As soon as she can feel the helmet with her foot, she kicks it as hard as possible. She feels her foot connect and kicks her assailant again. She can hear him stumble. She raises her gun up and comes face to face with the man, who is aiming his own pistol back at her.

They stay that way, locked in a stalemate. She hears a groan from Thomas. "Thomas, you okay?" she shouts without taking her eyes off the man in the helmet.

The man raises a mobile phone in his other hand. He types something into it and then shows her the screen. She reads 999. The phone rings until a voice picks up. "Hello, what is your emergency?"

"Uh," she pauses, trying to organize her thoughts. "Someone's hurt. Real bad," she says, trying to skip the fact that a brief shootout has occurred. "We need an ambulance right now. Please."

"What's the address?"

"We're on 66 St. John Street. Please, my friend is bleeding. We've, we've just had — a robbery. He's been shot."

"Ma'am? A robbery —"

The man in the helmet shuts his phone, ending the conversation. He puts away his gun, takes a notepad and a pen from the inside pocket of his jacket, and starts scribbling. He rips the paper off and passes it to Yunah. It reads "Soju Club, 7PM."

With that, he leaves.

CHAPTER 4

The Northerner

STANDING IN THE MIDDLE OF GLOUCESTER GREEN, Yohan chews on a kebab wrap purchased from a nearby stand while watching people stream out of the double-decker buses that have just arrived at the terminal. Several bus passengers get into the waiting cabs, while the majority stroll to their destinations with certainty in their gaits. After the crowd thins out, he mostly sees stragglers and tourists lingering in the square.

Nearby, there is a young American woman, blond, maybe in her late twenties or early thirties. He recognizes her from the dossier at the Magpie. She is looking at a paper map as she walks blindly into Yohan. He lets her slam right into him and pretends to flail a bit.

"Oh! Sorry."

"No problem."

"Actually, if you don't mind, can I ask you something?" she chirps. Her voice is high pitched, her mood overly optimistic.

He nods, then clears his throat after he swallows the bite in his mouth. "Sure."

"See, I need to get to this bed and breakfast, and I'm trying to find the best way to get there."

He takes a look at the map and realizes it is close to the Magpie. Maybe a couple of doors down on St. Clement's. "It's simple: you just get on High Street, and then you go all the way down until you cross the bridge."

"This bridge?" she points to the wrong bridge.

"No, this one. Magdalen Bridge."

"Ah, I see."

Doha's instructions regarding situations in engaging members of the public are based on two simple doctrines: no one spits at a smiling face and the nail that sticks out gets hammered down. Essentially, a combination of politeness and a general lack of words.

"So I just go all the way, and then what?" she asks, still pretending to be clueless.

He wonders what her gambit is, what she is hoping to get out of this. Perhaps she has others closing in on him while distracting him, but he sees no one in the periphery. He remembers Dr. Ryu's lessons: "These westerners, they're not like us. They are straightforward, they are unafraid to talk to anyone, and they say whatever they want. So keep things simple. Keep your answers short and always try to disengage as naturally as possible. And always remember politeness is your best camouflage. A single frown, a moment of disrespect. This is what people will recall the most. I've had an operative ignore a server while tracking a mark in a restaurant. Security agents later identified him because the server remembered him for being so rude."

So he puts up a smile. "You know what? I'm walking in that direction. Why don't you follow me?"

The girl's face brightens up. He pops the last bite of his kebab into his mouth and starts down the road.

"You from around here?" she asks as they walk side by side.

"I'm a student here," Yohan says, thinking he should stick to being Junichi. Perhaps she already knows who he is. There is no need to take the mask off.

"What are you studying?"

"Economics." This is partially true. His relationship with the faculty has mostly been managed by Doha, who had an extensive network in the university and lived fully in the light, unlike Dr. Ryu.

"Me too. I studied it in college."

She then goes off about her college experience, which all blurs into background noise, though he picks up that she finished her bachelor's degree and is taking a break for a year. Yohan glances over, knowing how old she really is and that this is all a cover.

"Western aeminai, they mature quite quickly. It's astonishing really. You think a girl is twenty-five and you find out she's only sixteen. It is like they're impatient to start their lives," Doha once said to him as they were drinking in a bar in Barcelona while monitoring a target.

Yohan hopes that she does not ask too many questions, not just because saying more than necessary is a hazard but also because he really hasn't been listening. At some point the talking stops. The girl's eyes are fixed on a masonry clock tower, topped off with a set of battlements. "What's that?" she asks.

"It's called the Carfax Tower."

She takes a minute to snap photos of the tower and then turns to Yohan to ask if he can take a photo of her.

"How do you do this? Is it this button?" He feigns ignorance, smirking shyly; he is very familiar with cameras for surveillance work.

"No, it's this button right there."

"This button?"

"Yes, that one."

She poses, her arms spread toward the sky.

"Always helps to fumble a bit," Doha used to say. "It is better to be underestimated. Be more by being less. Meekness is a shield behind which you can carry out your plans uninterrupted."

"One, two ... Sorry, I pressed the wrong one. I'll try again." After taking a few shots, Yohan passes the camera to the girl, who checks it and nods in approval.

From the tower it's more or less a simple line all the way down High Street and past Magdalen Bridge. It's quite a stretch, and Yohan glances around for the other agent, wondering if they're making a play here. Nothing happens during their long walk. When they finally reach the bed and breakfast, Yohan moves in for a simple handshake. Instead she comes in for a hug. "Hope to see you around," she says, smiling as she lets him go.

Just like that, he has successfully disengaged. Any other time, Doha would have congratulated him on not revealing anything about himself. In all that time, he didn't even have to divulge a name. He was flawlessly invisible.

However, he did feel her hand briefly scurry around his coat collar when she hugged him. He walks away, and once he is out of sight of the building, he takes his coat off and flips up the collar to find a small grey patch stuck underneath. For a moment, he thinks about taking the bug off. The doctrine dictates that every single risk factor must be eliminated unless instructed otherwise. Doha's lessons on Americans come back to him. It may be better that the Americans know where he is at all times. It would be like a shield protecting him against other threats. He leaves it. He flips the collar back down, puts the coat back on, and disappears into the streets again.

•

On the twelfth week of his assignment in Paris, Yohan meets with Dr. Ryu at a café near the ops centre he had set up in a hotel room. It is a routine checkup, once a week for monitoring purposes. They gather at a different café each time, at a different hour.

Opposite him, Dr. Ryu, her neck wrapped in a linen scarf, focuses on writing in her notepad on the table while Yohan sips coffee, casually scanning the street with his sunglasses on. When she is done, she looks up and smiles. "How are you feeling?" she asks in French.

"Good," he responds, also in French.

"Have you been doing your daily tasks?"

"Yes."

"Can you recite them to me?" she asks as she jots a few more notes down.

"Wake up, eat, practise the viola, go to classes, talk to the conductor after class and suggest a drink. If he accepts, then go along; if he doesn't accept, try again in a week."

"Has he accepted?"

"Not yet."

"Has he said anything?"

"He said he was busy."

She writes something in her notes. Yohan takes a sip of his coffee. A man and a woman walk by with a child in the middle, attracting his attention. The child looks up at the woman, holding her hand, naively smiling. The man, his arms filled with grocery bags, looks down to his son, tells him something, and then they're all laughing. The click of Dr. Ryu's pen brings him back to the conversation.

"How's your health? Are you eating the right number of calories?"

"Three thousand calories. Every day."

"Are you sticking to the nutrition plan I gave you?"

"Yes."

"Alcohol consumption?"

"Three glasses of wine a day."

"How do you feel after drinking?"

"Sober."

"Very good."

Her espresso has been untouched for a while. She picks it up, tastes it, and frowns. She turns to a passing server and asks for another.

"Are you keeping up with your daily training?"

"Yes."

"Can I see your logbook?"

Yohan pulls out a notebook from a briefcase by his feet. She takes it and reads it while another cup of espresso arrives. Yohan thanks the server in Dr. Ryu's stead while she pores over the pages.

"You missed a run here."

"I woke up late that day."

"Why?"

"I went to bed late the night before. I was out with a classmate."

"And was this classmate male or female?"

"Female."

"Ethnicity?"

"French."

"What sort of French?"

"White."

"I see." She puts the notebook down and observes Yohan for a while. She picks up her cup, sips from it, all the while not taking her eyes off him. "So you're telling me you went out into the city with a person who had no strategic value, and because of that, you disrupted your routine, resulting in a lapse."

Yohan feels tense. He does not want to be scrutinized for every minute of his life. He feels like he is being cut open, his intestines taken out and displayed on the table for her to carefully examine.

"Do you have urges?" she says after a pause.

Yohan shakes his head. "No, no, I don't."

"Do you need me to assign you someone to relieve yourself?"

"No."

"Then why did you go out with this woman?"

Yohan tries to think back to the day when a striking blond girl in a blouse and a black knee-length skirt, who had been his stand partner for weeks, asked him if he wanted to go out for a glass of wine. During practice, their hands would brush against each other when they both reached to turn the page.

"Why did you go out with this woman?" Dr. Ryu calmly repeats.

"She asked me."

"Why didn't you say no?"

"I did, but she asked me again."

Dr. Ryu leans in, her arms folded. "I just want to know your reasoning. That is all."

"She said just one drink. Just one. And I knew that my daily intake should be three, so I thought, Why not? I wasn't making any progress with the professor that week anyway. She took me to a bar where we had some wine."

"Go on," she asks. "What did you talk about?"

"She asked me where I was from, and I told her that I moved from Hong Kong at a young age. She told me that she was from Bordeaux, where her family has a farm. We talked about the class and how she was hoping to make it into an orchestra one day. She asked me what music I enjoy, so I told her that I like Mahler and Shostakovich. She said she likes them, too, but she actually enjoys jazz more. So we went to see a jazz band. And then we strolled along the Seine, and she showed me the Notre Dame cathedral at night. Around then I noticed that I was past my curfew, so we went back. She wanted to come up, but I said no. Before I could leave, she pulled me by my collar and kissed me."

"She kissed you on the lips?"

"Yes."

"How did you feel about it?"

He tries to recall that night, when the girl wrapped her arms around him and he was powerless as she slipped her tongue into his mouth. It was all so new and foreign. "It was strange."

"I see."

A man on a scooter goes by, dressed in a suit and a bright red helmet. The loud muffler interrupts them, but Dr. Ryu quickly turns her attention back to him. "Yohan, I'm not going to report any of this to anyone, including Commander Kim. I'm also going to tell you that what you did was reckless. You should not have talked to her under any circumstances. Only focus on the target."

"Yes, I'm sorry."

"I'm pulling you off the assignment. You are to hand over your case file on the conductor and I will give it to a new agent."

"What will you tell them? What will be the official reason?"

She smiles and grabs his hand, squeezing it gently. He suddenly feels the tension drain from him. Her kindness washes over him, and he sighs.

"There is nothing to worry about, Yohan. I will take care of everything. As long as you listen to me, you are safe."

It is a disappointment to hear all this, especially after he has put all this effort into the mission. But this is part of the job. He must always be ready to leave each and every place. He must never allow himself to be comfortable anywhere and he must never connect with anyone. He feels uneasy at this thought but smiles for Dr. Ryu. All he can do is believe her. He has done that all his life and she has never led him astray.

"Yes, Dr. Ryu."

The Southerner

"I'm done with this batch of kimchi. Anything else?" Deoksu calls out from the kitchen.

"Come help me out here," Jihoon shouts back.

Deoksu comes out to the hall, pulling off the plastic gloves covered with thick red sauce. A crowd of Korean tourists have come in for lunch, filling every single table. The hall is instantly full of raucous conversations among elderly Koreans armed with fanny packs, sun visors, and expensive cameras hanging around their necks. While Jihoon is used to these sorts of lunch rushes, it doesn't help that they scheduled their monthly gimjang for today. Deoksu jumps into action swiftly, helping to bring out dishes that were supposed to go out a while ago. Jihoon goes out to serve more banchan and apologize for the delay, but the tourists are in a good mood. Some of them tell him that he reminds them of their grandson.

Jihoon does not mind these chaotic moments, and often he feels at ease with them. Whenever Korean tourists come, he feels transported to his mother's restaurant. The tiny establishment would burst at the seams with office workers and labourers. The dining section of the restaurant was just a raised matted area, where customers sat on floor cushions with tables between them. Jihoon would have to step over people's legs to serve the tables in the far corner. Shoes littered the entrance. It was disorganized, disorienting, and warm.

"Wa, ssibal — I feel like I'm going to lose my mind," Deoksu says as he comes back from serving a tray full of bowls of kimchi jjigae and haejang guk. "It's crazy, these old timers are chugging soju like it's water. This will at least be a week's worth of normal business."

"Well, I don't want them to get too drunk," Jihoon muses as he fills up yet another tray of banchan. "I'd like them to be able to walk out of here on their own feet."

In the middle of the throng, he spots Junichi through the window, looking into the restaurant. Jihoon serves the side dishes he is holding and goes to the door to greet him. "Hey, want to come in to eat?"

"Seems busy."

"A bit, yes."

"Got a table?"

"For you alone? No. Unless you don't mind sharing a table."

Junichi thinks for a bit. "I don't mind that at all."

This surprises Jihoon and he leads Junichi all the way to the back, where there is one seat left at a small table with two elderly Korean men.

"Hello there, sirs. Would you mind sharing this table with this gentleman here? He is a regular of mine and —"

"Of course, of course! Bring him over. Come on!"

Jihoon puts his thumb up and points to the empty chair; Junichi sits. The table has a wide pot of bubbling budae jjigae, filled with meats, vegetables, and ramen noodles, all above a small square-shaped butane gas stove.

"Hello there! Chonggak!" says the man to Junichi's left, in Korean. His hair is completely grey, his wrinkles deeply etching into the edges of his eyes as he smiles brightly beneath his oversized visor.

"No, no, he's not Korean. He's, uh, he's Japanese," Jihoon says.

"Japanese?" the man with the visor asks loudly, turning to the man to Junichi's right, who is sporting a moustache and a bright neon windbreaker zipped up to his neck. "Of course, Korea's better. But Japan's a good place to visit. We were there last month!"

"Oh yes. One of our best trips."

"Where are you from? We had the most exquisite okonomiyaki in Hiroshima!"

Despite Jihoon telling them Junichi doesn't speak Korean, the old men continue talking in their language. As if it will all somehow get through to him.

"He's not from Japan," Jihoon says as he lays down a small plate and utensils in front of Junichi. "He's French."

"French? He's French? He's not French!" the moustached man exclaims.

"Ah, why are you so backwards? He can be French! Just as I can be American if I go to America," the man with the visor says.

"That's not what I'm saying. What I'm saying is what you're inside, you know?" The moustached man pounds his chest with his palm. "That never changes. I mean you can take me out of my country, but you can't take kimchi out of me. I'll crave it wherever I go!"

"Pardon my friend, he's had a bit too much to drink," the man with the visor says. "You, stop with the soju."

"Let me be! My sons are all grown up, I've got nothing I need to do anymore! I'm done! All I've got left is to see more of this world until I die."

Junichi seems amused rather than irritated. Jihoon gives him a menu, but the man with the visor waves him off. "Nonsense! Put that away, we can share this budae jjigae," he says as he takes an empty bowl and scoops out a portion of the stew still simmering above the blue flames.

"It's all right. This looks good," Junichi says to Jihoon as the two old men continue to banter jovially in Korean while scooping food into a bowl.

"Jal-meok-get-seum-nida," Junichi says in a surprisingly smooth pronunciation. The old men are at first stunned, and then they laugh.

"So you do speak Korean," the moustached man chuckles as he slaps Junichi's back.

From then on, Junichi switches to fluent Korean with them. For a moment, Jihoon's eyes meet Junichi's, and the restaurateur tries not to act surprised. Of course, it's possible that he speaks Korean. Nowadays people who aren't Korean seem to speak Korean all the time. The other day, there was a

British man who brought his Korean date and ordered in fluent Korean. Deoksu thought it was nauseating and he secretly spat in the man's stew, but Jihoon thought nothing of it.

When the tourists eventually file out, happily stumbling into the streets as they sing old Korean trot medleys, Jihoon and Deoksu start to clean up the place, stacking dirty plates and carrying them back to the kitchen. Junichi watches and suddenly decides to help as well, picking up the soju bottles from the table he's sitting at.

"You don't need to do that," Jihoon comments, but Junichi continues.

Once the tables have been cleared, Junichi sits down, seemingly in thought.

"You got some room for more drinks?" Jihoon asks as he joins him.

Junichi nods. Jihoon goes to the back and picks out two clean soju glasses. He takes out a bottle from the cooler, holds it by the neck, and swirls it around before suddenly stopping. The liquid inside forms a whirlpool that stretches from the top to the middle of the bottle.

"That's neat," Junichi points.

"It's a good trick, yeah."

"Does it do anything for it?"

"No, it just looks cool."

Jihoon opens the cap with a sharp twist. The aluminum seal cracks, leaving a circular trail as he lifts it up. He pours two shots. They raise their glasses, meet them in the middle, and drink.

"You never said you spoke Korean," Jihoon says as he pours more soju for himself and Junichi.

"I've learned a few words here and there."

"That wasn't just a few words back there. You speak other languages?"

"French. Chinese. Russian," Junichi says, pausing after each one.

"That's quite a lot. I just know some English."

"I find that's the one that gets the most done, anyway."

"How did you learn all those languages?"

Junichi ponders, looking at the soju glass. "My parents moved around for their jobs, and whenever we went to a new place, they thought it was important for me to learn the local language. To be aware of what's going on."

"And what did they do?"

"Academics. Literature professors. They still are."

"My mother studied literature. She stopped before graduating because she couldn't afford it. She had me and she wanted to focus on raising me right." Jihoon feels as if something is closing around his chest as he says this. He pours another pair of shots.

"She never went back to school to finish?" Junichi asks.

Jihoon wants to change the subject, but he can't think of how to do it without being impolite. "No. She was working night and day. To provide me a better future. There was no time."

"What did she do?"

"Ran a restaurant. Just like this one."

"Nice." Junichi pauses, then continues. "You said she wanted to give you a better future. What do you think that future looked like to her?"

"I don't know, working at a desk maybe?"

They laugh.

"Has she seen this place? It's awesome. Trust me. My professor and I, we've been to many places in Europe. No Korean restaurant has been as good as this one."

"Well, she's too far away. I don't think she'll ever see it."

"I'm sure your mother is proud of you."

Jihoon feels something well up in him. He drinks his shot without waiting for Junichi, who follows suit. He breathes in through his teeth, feeling the liquor go down with a slight burn. Jihoon moves to pour another round, but this time, there is only enough left for a half shot each. It's the last shot.

"You see here, Jihoon, a bottle of soju has seven shots, which means you always have to order another one." He remembers his mother's words: "Let's say you have two people. They drink, but one will eventually be left out. Now you have to order another one because you can't take a shot by yourself. Even with three people, you have only one left after two rounds. With four people, there's not enough after one round, and so on and so forth. No one ever drinks only one round of soju. Ever. This is important for us because it means we sell more."

Jihoon suggested that it evened out when two people drink two bottles. But his mother said once a pair goes through two soju bottles, they will inevitably go for more. It was the law of good times, or so she said. Perhaps these were the real teachings that mattered. Not what he painstakingly memorized and studied at school for the sake of acing an exam.

Jihoon splits the seventh shot and they finish the bottle.

"Thanks for the drinks and food, as always," Junichi says, standing up. "I'll be back later."

"With your professor this time?"

"No, I'm afraid he won't be able to make it tonight. It'll be just me."

Jihoon nods. They shake hands and exchange smiles. Soon after Junichi leaves, Deoksu also departs, after he has prepped everything for the next day. Jihoon reminds himself to put up a help wanted flyer soon. He'll need someone to take over for Deoksu. This time he'll add that being Korean is a requirement. Perhaps that will narrow down the pool this time. Besides, if Jihoon has learned anything with Deoksu, it's that it helps to be with someone who speaks the language. It's just easier, more comforting, even. There's just a way that a sentence strung together in Korean makes him feel that he never gets from English. That is how Jihoon knows he is Korean, no matter how much he tries to leave it all behind.

•

The day before the exam, Jihoon comes home from a long day of practice tests. He feels ready. When he arrives his mother has a small table out with a soju bottle and two small glasses. He sits right across from her, setting his bag down next to him.

He has never had a drink in his life. He has heard of his more carefree classmates going out to bars that secretly serve underage drinkers. The convenience store he works at stocks various brands. The most famous one, Chamiseul, the green bottle with the toad logo in the upper corner, is the one in front of Jihoon.

"Drinking is a big part of life. And I want you to learn it properly. Not from some older kid you'll meet in university. I don't want to get a call that you're in the hospital for alcohol poisoning. So I'm going to show you."

His mother twists the metal cap, which comes off with a sharp crackle. "First I will teach you the proper etiquette. There are rules to drink appropriately with others, and only then will you be able to climb through the ranks and make the right connections at school and work."

She passes the bottle to Jihoon, who takes it timidly, uncertain of what to do with it. He cradles it in his two hands, careful not to let the liquid spill over the bottle's mouth.

"Always the eldest first, then the second eldest. If the elder person offers to pour, always hold the glass with two hands and lower your gaze, like you're bowing." She holds out her glass with two hands, demonstrating how it is done. "When you toast, your glass must be lower than the elder person's."

"What if there's a group of people?"

"Then just make sure you go as low as possible. Just to be safe."

Jihoon does as he is told and puts the upper edge of the glass near the lower end of his mother's. It makes a crisp sound when the two gently touch, and they each pull their shots back.

"Now, when you drink with an elder, never face the elder when you drink. Instead turn your face to the side, along with your shot, and then just take it all in." His mother demonstrates again, turning once to show how he should do it.

Following her lead, he drinks. "It's very harsh," he says as he frowns, wincing at how the soju scrapes against his throat as it goes down. He wonders where the heat he feels burning against his insides is coming from when the bottle is so cold.

"A lot of people like it because it's harsh and coarse. People like the sensation. You will come to enjoy it."

Sometimes he would stop by the restaurant after his shift at the convenience store. The restaurant would be closed, but his mother would be there still, sitting at a table with an assortment of banchan and a lone bottle of soju. With her shoulders sagging and her head hung heavily from fatigue, she looked numb as she picked through the food with her chopsticks. He wonders if that is what she means by enjoying the drink. It silences the noise.

"Eomma, I'm sorry. I should've let you know about working at the convenience store," he says, feeling that his apology is belated but necessary.

"It's okay. I'm okay that you work there. I trust your judgment."

She leans in to pour another shot, and remembering what he has been taught, Jihoon hastily holds up the glass with two hands.

"I'm proud of you," his mother says as she lets the soju stream over the mouth of the bottle. "You've grown up so well. I was always worried that I wasn't giving you enough, that I wasn't providing enough. But now that I see you, you've proven all of that wrong. Thank you, Jihoon."

He puts his glass below hers as she brings it across the table to meet his. A gentle touch, and he turns his head to the side and drinks it, holding the shot with his two hands the entire time.

"You'll be the first to go to university in our family. I never thought I could make that happen. All this time, I thought that I was robbing you of the opportunity because I couldn't afford to send you to hagwons like the other kids. But I see now, you are a son that I don't deserve."

Jihoon wants to tell her the truth. He does not want any of this. Going to university for a degree that everyone says will be very useful and then getting a job at a company that everyone says will be secure. What he wants, in fact, is far simpler. He wants to stay with his mother at the restaurant. They can work as mother and son, feeding customers day and night. They will save up money and get an even bigger restaurant, which will enable them to save even more. Each summer, he will take her on a vacation in Europe, a place she has loved to read about in books but has never seen in person. But saying that he doesn't want to go to university would surely break her. And for that, Jihoon stays quiet and can only accept another drink, just as he has learned.

On the morning of the great exam, Jihoon's mother walks with him to school. She is dressed elegantly in a pleated long skirt and a white blouse with a cardigan. She is holding his lunch, which is wrapped in a multicolored bojagi bundle and tied nicely on top in the shape of a bow. In front of the school, there is a gauntlet of junior high schoolers holding up signs like "Sunbaedeul fighting!" and "Suneung daebak-nasaeyo!" cheering the third-year students as they go through the gates to sit for their exam. It will be the most nerve-wracking event in their entire lives. Their adulthood will be essentially decided by this exam. At least that is what their parents, their teachers, and their peers have been telling them.

"Here you go, son." She passes him the bundle when they arrive at the school gate. "Rice, mackerel jorim, namul, siraegi guk, and kimchi."

It is still warm. Freshly made early in the morning. He can feel the heat through the cloth.

"I'm going to spend some time in the city, do some errands. I'll come back when your exam is done."

"Thanks, Eomma," he says, hugging the bundle close to his chest.

"Good luck," she says. "Now go. You don't want to be late."

He walks through the gate and looks back repeatedly. Each time he looks, she is there. He passes through the main doors of the school and disappears inside.

When the exam is finished, the sun is beginning to set, alighting the sky orange. Jihoon can't even remember what he wrote on the exam or anything he had learned for it for that matter. Looking around as he walks down the corridor, he notices that others feel the same. They are all empty faced, as if they have survived a bombing. The lunch bundle is still with him. He contemplated eating it, but he figured a full stomach would mess with his concentration. Perhaps it was the adrenalin, but he could not feel any hunger.

Students exiting the gate are greeted by their parents. Some hug their mothers and fathers in triumph, though many break down in tears as soon as they see their loved ones' expectant looks. Jihoon looks around the gate but does not see his mother. He hopes that she is not too irritated about the uneaten lunch. He hopes the news of his exam having gone well will make her happy. He sits on a curb and watches the other students go home from their ordeal.

An hour goes by, and Jihoon's mother does not show. He tries calling her, but she does not answer her phone. He wants to go look for her, but he knows that she always does as she promises, and she promised to meet him at school after the exam. He has made a dinner reservation for them at an Italian restaurant renowned for its pasta. In all their years of running a restaurant, he cannot remember a time when he and his mother were served a meal. At dinner he has a plan to surprise her with a trip to Europe.

After waiting for another hour, he starts to feel hunger creeping in. He decides that it may be a good time to eat the lunch bundle. Just as he is working on untying the bow, he gets a call. When he hears what the voice on the other line says, he hurriedly runs to the closest main street, waves down a cab, and asks for the nearby hospital.

Once he arrives he rushes to the reception desk and tells them his mother's name. A nurse takes him to a waiting room by the surgery suite. She explains what happened. His mother was crossing a road when a silver Mercedes sedan sped around the corner and hit her, sending her flying over the car and landing behind it as it drove off frantically with a skid. An onlooker called an ambulance, and his mother was immediately brought here. She is now in surgery, and he has to wait until further notice.

An hour passes, and he feels hungry again. He thinks of the dosirak his mother had packed him. He looks around and realizes that he left the meal his mother had so carefully made for him back at the school gate. So he sits there, starving. He checks his watch and sees that it is thirty minutes past their dinner reservation.

The American

Sitting in the waiting room at John Radcliffe Hospital, Yunah writes then rewrites a message on her phone to explain to headquarters exactly what happened. She wonders just how much time she has before things fall apart even more. The story she gave the police won't add up. It'll be easy to find out that the gun Thomas dropped was not the robber's weapon.

She gives up on the message and takes out the note given to her by the man in the helmet. It's a rendezvous, but with whom she has no idea. It could be Dr. Ryu or perhaps even Junichi. But it could also be a trick. This could be a distraction to throw her off. Maybe Thomas is right about her. She just can't resist doing whatever it takes, going that extra bit because she knows she is in the right. She hopes he isn't hurt too badly. Despite their differences, she has always felt at ease around Thomas. He is someone she can rely on. There is a clear sense of give-and-take between the two of them, and outside of that, there are no expectations like there are with Koreans.

For the longest time, Yunah preferred to stay clear of Koreans. She found them to be two-faced fakers, ready to stab their own in the back with no notice. The first seeds of distrust were sown by a great betrayal when she was in middle school. On the eve of the opening of the family's bagel store, the employees — a small group of middle-aged Korean men her father had gotten to know through church — suddenly quit on him. Later, he found out through gossip that another churchgoer opening a franchise restaurant had poached them by offering them two dollars more per hour. But it wasn't just that. They waited until the day before the bagel store's opening to twist the knife. They wanted him to fail because they couldn't stand that a man younger than them was their employer.

Faced with the prospect of having to close, Yunah's father went to a local hardware store, where he heard he could find day labourers to work for him. There he picked up three Mexican workers who, like him, barely spoke a word of English. They were Manuel, Carlos, and Juan. Her father decided that he would call Manuel "Manu" because he found the last syllable difficult. They became his most reliable employees, holding the store together. Even her mother, who was stingy enough to take the bus if it meant saving on parking fees, never said a word of protest when it came to giving them raises. When Yunah started working there after an employee vacated the cashier position without notice, they became her tíos. They were the reason why she started taking Spanish classes and why she aced those exams, especially the speaking portions.

"Ssibal Koreans. Scumbags. Stabbing their own in the back," her father had said. "Never again. I'm never hiring Koreans again. Ssibal."

Despite this betrayal, Yunah still gave Koreans a chance because it was easy and convenient to be friends with them. On her first day of high school, a group of five second-generation Korean girls asked her if she was Korean. She nodded, and that was all that was required to join their clique. They would often hang out to share notes on exams and study at cafés and food courts. She was the smartest one of them all, always acing everything. Her friends relied on her. She felt good about that.

Things changed when she achieved a perfect score on the SAT. It was her mother who had proudly spread the word at church, and it eventually reached the girls. The shift didn't happen immediately, but conversations would be cut short and the invitations to hang out lessened. The girls would ask for class notes, but they didn't include her in conversations. Eventually, they cut her out altogether when she was the only one in the group accepted to an Ivy League school. At Harvard it was the same cutthroat competition with other Koreans and Yunah found it tiresome. With people like Thomas, there was none of that. He didn't try to best her or beat her. It was odd, but she felt more comfortable with him than with those whom she supposedly shared an identity with.

She thinks again about what to say to her handler, Cole. Something has to be said. While deep in thought about what words could get her in least trouble, she is informed by a nurse that Thomas has been moved to a bed and is taken to see him. Though unconscious, he is in a stable condition. She sits by Thomas, who is connected to a breathing tube along with a dozen other apparatus. She wishes he was awake so she could ask him whether he ever thought of her as a colleague and partner, not just someone to keep an eye on. Had any of those nights at the pub, when they were mopping vomit off the floor and telling off troublesome patrons, meant anything?

Her cellphone rings. She looks at the number and doesn't recognize it but decides to answer.

"Agent Choi, where are you?"

"Who's this?"

"Where are you?"

Yunah sighs. "I'm at the hospital with Thomas."

"What happened?"

"We got attacked."

"By whom?"

"I couldn't see who it was. He was wearing a motorcycle helmet and leather jacket. He ran off."

"Choi, I'm part of the relief team. You are to stay at the hospital with Manning. Do not leave his side until I arrive."

The call abruptly ends. She checks the time and sees that it is almost the hour to meet the mystery person at the Soju Club. She looks over to Thomas.

Thomas would say that she needs to stay put and do her duty as told. But she has done that all this time. She never said no, and she carried out her tasks with diligence and obedience. When she was relegated to paperwork for years, she didn't push back. She's never gone astray.

But this is where that has to stop. It's not disobedience. At least that's what she tells herself. This is the right thing to do. They don't know what she knows, and she knows better. For the sake of the mission, she must say no for once in her life.

So she leaves for the Soju Club.

CHAPTER 5

The Northerner

YOHAN WOULD HAVE STAYED AT THE SOJU CLUB LONGer, but he noticed a man passing the restaurant multiple times. He was bearded, dressed in a T-shirt and jeans with a hoodie. He was one of the two outlined in the dossier. As he talked with Jihoon, Yohan glanced through the window a few times to find the man either standing around the convenience store across the street, pretending to look through the gift card rack displayed outside, or simply walking past the restaurant with his eyes fixed forward.

After stepping out of the Soju Club, Yohan goes to the convenience store. He quickly picks out an energy drink and pays for it, ignoring the owner's attempt to make small talk, and then walks out, catching a good look at the man's face, almost making eye contact. The man reacts quickly, turning his head away, but Yohan has seen him already. He opens the can and takes a large gulp. He feels a bit of clarity kick in and the alcohol's effects slightly dissipate. He crosses the street, and the bearded man follows him at a distance.

Something has changed. They have never been this assertive. The Americans only ever kept watch from a distance, or in the case of the Magpie, opted to wait until Yohan approached. Of course, Doha's death may have been a trigger for an escalation, but Yohan does not know what they have planned for him.

"There is a rationale to everything," Doha once said. "When something seems out of order, it is usually an effect of a cause. Nothing is random. So if you see your enemies do something unusual, you must find out why that is happening. Or get the hell out of there at least."

So Yohan takes a moment to think as he continues to sip the energy drink and keep the man in his periphery. He throws the empty can in the trash, crosses the street, and prepares to make his move. Assuming this is an American agent, he cannot use violence. He merely needs to talk to him as Junichi and try to get any detail that may give hints to the current situation.

The bearded man walks into a café to the left, so Yohan does the same. He stands next to him while the man orders. When it is his turn, Yohan orders a macchiato, and as he waits, he senses the man glancing at him. He catches his eye, and the man smiles in return without saying anything. When the man's drink is ready, he walks to the counter to take it, then walks up to Yohan. He braces himself to either fight the man or run.

"We want to talk to you," says the man. "Yes or no?"

"Who wants to talk to me?"

"Yes or no?"

Yohan hears his name being called. The man promptly goes to the counter in Yohan's stead, retrieves the small cup of macchiato, and hands it to him. Yohan takes a sip, not taking his eyes off the man. "Yes," he finally says.

The man leads him back to the Magpie. Once inside, Yohan looks around to find the place nearly empty. Seonhye is nowhere in sight, and he doesn't see the other bartender. He finds the blond tourist woman from earlier sitting at the bar. The man turns around and pats him down. When done, he pulls at Yohan's backpack, which he gives up easily. He throws the backpack to the blond at the bar. She gestures to a seat at a nearby table. "Feel free to sit." Yohan does as he's told.

"Hands on the table," the bearded man adds. Yohan puts both of his hands on the table, palms down.

"No, no, let's relax. This isn't an interrogation. This is a negotiation," the blond says as she approaches. "Thanks for the directions earlier. You knew, right? That's why you stood there, waiting for me. I knew it and you knew it, so let's cut the charade."

The blond woman sits across from him, playfully dangling her crossed legs. Yohan reminds himself that he has no reason to say anything. Whether an interrogation or negotiation, Doha has taught him that silence is what breaks down the opponent's resolve. With absolutely no feedback, the interrogator is unable to make progress, allowing Yohan to take partial control of the situation.

The blond woman opens his backpack and starts to pour out the contents. Passports, driver's licences, and paper permits all spill onto the table. She goes through them one by one. "So many names. Such a grand effort for — I don't know. What are you accomplishing here, exactly? What did you get done?"

She pulls out a stack of photos from her pocket. One by one, she places them on the table and pushes them toward

Yohan. They are bodies and faces. All of them are dead. "You recognize them?"

Yohan nods. He knows the locations of all the photographs. He had visited each operative when they were still alive. The blond tips her head in curiosity, intrigued by his steady and quiet demeanour.

"You understand what's going on, right?" she says, pointing to the photos strewn across the table in front of him. "You're being liquidated. They don't need you anymore. Regime change: they want a new set of toys that they can control. You're past your expiry date."

Yohan still does not say anything. If it is the republic's will, he must accept it. At least on the surface.

She stands up, walks behind him, and puts her hand on his shoulder. "Don't worry, I'm not doing anything you wouldn't like." She tucks her hand under his coat collar and removes the bug. She puts it on the tip of her finger and shows it to him. "See this? Now it's off. A bit of good will. Because unlike them, we want what's best for you. Work with us. Choose anywhere in the United States to live. New York, Los Angeles, Seattle, San Francisco. We'll give you a nice sum of money every month. Enough to afford a great place, eat good food, and live a comfortable life. How does that sound?"

Yohan imagines such a life. He thinks about Boston and recalls what Doha said about the city. Perhaps he can go to school there, find something to study and live the American dream.

From behind, the blond gently combs through his hair with her fingers. Yohan clenches his hands into fists, trying to hold in his discomfort. "What are you really fighting for? Why fight, even? There's no need. It's time for a break, no?"

She sits down next to him on the edge of the table, her legs brushing against his arm. For a moment, they stare at each other. The blond thinks she knows what's best for him. She thinks she has the power in this exchange and is offering something of value to him. It's almost like mercy.

Yohan is reminded of another lesson from Doha: "Whenever you notice arrogance in your enemies, seep into them like water entering the cracks of a rock and break them from within. Let them be blind to your eventual and inevitable threat."

"What do you want in return?" he asks.

The blond nods, smiling. "I know the person you're waiting for. Your boss."

"My boss is gone."

"Your other boss. We know he's coming. We know you're going to meet him."

This elicits a response, a sudden jerk of his head. It's not that he is surprised they know about Dr. Ryu's arrival. It is that they have evidently never seen Dr. Ryu and think she is a man.

"Ah, you *are* waiting." The blond pulls her head back in satisfaction, keeping her eyes trained on Yohan. "Look, you're young, you're smart, and frankly, you're quite handsome." She smiles and the bearded one scoffs. "You'll be just at home with us back in America. You could be anything there. You could have a great life. We'll give you the chance to do that. All you need to do is help us with this small thing."

The bearded man seems to receive a call on his earpiece and interrupts the blond. "Cops have been called to their flat," he says.

"Cops? For what?"

"Manning. He's been shot."

•

Yohan wakes up to Doha frantically shaking him. "Get up, get up!"

"What's going on?" Yohan sits up in bed. It is still dark outside. They have been ordered to lie low until cleared to leave. The police have been on high alert since the hit from two nights ago. It was a quick job. He wore a helmet and rode a scooter, following a convoy of SUVs that crawled out of the South Korean embassy in Brussels. At a red right, he sidled up to the second car. Four shots through the rear passenger window and the defector was dead. The scooter was abandoned and the gun was thrown in a river. But Doha decided it would be wise to stay put until the heat died down.

Yohan feels disoriented. He figures that he got around eight hours of sleep, which is plenty relative to what he usually gets. Yet he feels more tired than usual. Looking around, it takes him a bit of time to remember where he is. The ceiling, with its curves and antique details, reminds him that they're in a hotel.

"Follow me; we're going outside," Doha says. Yohan quickly changes into a pair of jeans, a white T-shirt, and a black down jacket. Just as he moves to pick up his phone, Doha stops him by grabbing his hand. "Don't bring that."

They stop at the door, and Doha turns to Yohan, face to face. "We're going to get in a cab. We're going to Brussels Nord station. When the cab stops for a red light at an intersection nearby, you're going to get out of the cab and enter the train station. Inside the train station, go to platform two. There you'll meet someone. You will know who it is."

The cab arrives in front of the hotel. Doha tells the driver to head toward Docks Bruxsel, a mall. As planned, when the car stops at a red light, Yohan gets out. He enters the train station, nearly vacant at this early hour. He climbs the stairs to platform two, and there he finds a woman sitting, waiting for the train. He briefly reads the sign. It is heading to Berlin. The woman turns her head, takes her sunglasses off, and motions him over. It is Dr. Ryu.

"Come," she says. "Sit next to me."

Yohan does as she tells him.

"Goodness," she says, softly turning Yohan's face left and right with her fingers. "You look exhausted. You're sleeping too much."

"There's not much else to do."

"I told Doha to give you enough to keep yourself occupied. Too much sleep is not good."

"I'm okay."

"Are you?" She leans her head against her fist, her elbow resting on the edge of the backrest.

"Yes," Yohan says confidently, hoping to assure her.

"I'll be away for a while. I wanted to tell you in person."

"Where are you going?"

"Home. I've been called back, it seems."

Yohan feels a tingle run up his back. Home never calls unless there is a problem. It is their duty to allow the motherland to sleep in peace. He can't help but think that this may be the last time he sees her. He looks around instinctively, but Dr. Ryu puts her hand on his shoulder. "It's okay. It's just us here. Doha has made sure of it."

"What's my part in this?"

"You have no part. We're going to take care of all of it."

"We?"

"Doha and me. You don't need to worry."

"Can I do anything?"

"No, Yohan. Trust Doha. Do as he says."

Yohan nods.

"If he asks you to do something and you don't understand, just remember it will all make sense in the end."

Yohan nods again.

"And whatever you do, Yohan, stay alive."

The loudspeaker announces that a train is arriving.

"It's time for you to go." She gets up, but Yohan does not. Dr. Ryu looks down at him. "Is something wrong?"

"Doha won't tell me anything. I'm told to do this and told to do that, but no one explains to me what's going on."

Dr. Ryu sits back down. She holds his face in her hands and looks into his eyes. Her gaze has always been gentle toward Yohan, even when she punished him. "I know it troubles you. All of this fog. You have to trust us. We have never failed you. You know that."

Yohan nods.

"Next time we see each other, it will all make sense. I promise you. But for now, you have to put your faith in us. We would never lead you astray."

The train is arriving. Its lights shine brighter as it gets closer. Both stand up and face each other as the train passes them by, fluttering their hair in its wake. When the train finally stops and it is quiet again, Dr. Ryu looks up at him. "You've grown so tall. I feel I never stopped to appreciate how well you've turned out." She slowly lifts her hand up. Yohan waits for her to reach out, but she stops. Instead she balls her hand into a fist and places it on her chest. "Take care of him. Doha. He puts so much on his own shoulders and forgets that he is only human. Out here he's just like any of us. Expendable, vulnerable."

"I will."

"And take care of yourself."

She enters the closest train car, and just as she finds a seat, the train starts to move. He barely has enough time to wave goodbye to her through the window of the train.

Back in the cab, Doha asks him whether anyone else was there. Yohan answers it was just him and Dr. Ryu.

"Good. No word of this. Ever. You didn't meet Dr. Ryu tonight. I didn't take you out. The story is that she was gone by the time we got back to Oxford. If anyone from home calls and asks, that's what you answer. You understand?"

Yohan nods and wonders what the point of this rendezvous was. But he knows that he is not supposed to ask questions, ever. He is simply glad that he was able to see Dr. Ryu for one last time.

The Southerner

Once he is alone in the restaurant, Jihoon takes the opportunity to eat, just as his mother had taught him. It is best to try to take care of your own meals when there is no customer to watch you eat. Jihoon decides to put together a quick bibimbap bowl from leftovers.

After a few mouthfuls, he hears a bell and the front door opening. He looks up as an Asian woman walks in. At first glance, the woman could be in her forties or even fifties. She has short black hair with parted bangs, one side draping over her wrinkleless forehead. She has high cheekbones and a striking pointed nose. She is wearing a long red pleated skirt and a loose white blouse, the sleeves cut just past the elbows. A navy trench coat is hanging from her forearm.

Quickly, he puts his spoon down, takes a napkin to wipe his mouth, and stands to approach her. "Hello. Table for one?"

"Yes, please," she says. "Table for one." Her English is slightly accented, reminding him of the old professor. Subtle dullness around the *r* and *l*. It gives her a sense of nobility. Her voice is calm and her words are clear. He wonders if she is Korean.

Jihoon leads her to a small table opposite from where he is having his meal. She sets down her coat on one of the chairs and sits facing the street. Jihoon hands her a menu. "If you don't mind, I'm just finishing my meal here. But please let me know when you're ready to order."

"Thank you." She smiles warmly and starts perusing the menu.

Jihoon tries to eat quickly so he can head back to the kitchen for his newest customer. His mother used to tell him to slow down whenever he was late for his early morning classes. She would say that wherever he needed to get to could wait. She wanted him to take his time, chew and enjoy his food.

"Excuse me," he hears when he begins to see the bottom of his bowl. "What is that? What are you eating there?"

"Bibimbap."

"May I have that?"

"Sure."

Jihoon goes back to the kitchen and starts to prepare her meal. On top of a packed base of rice, he carefully arranges the ingredients so that they form a wheel of colour. He adds a fried egg, cooked sunny side up so the yellow yolk is right in the middle. He scoops some gochujang sauce into a small bowl and then serves everything on a tray, with utensils.

"Thank you," she says and then pauses as if in thought. "I'll also take a bottle of soju," she finally says.

Jihoon promptly serves a green bottle of soju along with one small glass. Soju and bibimbap. Jihoon finds this combination odd. Though soju goes well with everything, whether it is jjigae, pajeon, or a plate of sliced raw fish served with a piece of lemon and a side of soy sauce and wasabi. He has had soju with pizza. There is no right way to do it as long as you're enjoying it.

Seeing that the woman is satisfied with her food and drink, Jihoon lets her know that he'll just be outside if he needs her. He steps out the front, lights a cigarette, and takes a deep drag. At night Oxford becomes quiet. The vibrancy of the day brought by students and tourists is subdued, its energy sapped as the city prepares itself for slumber.

Except the first time he visited, Jihoon has never explored Oxford much. He has never had a chance to really look around other than a superficial sweep of the university campus and the city that surrounds it. There are places to go, he assumes, but he has stayed in the restaurant. Within the four walls of the Soju Club, he feels at ease while making food and serving customers. He enjoys the comfort of feeding others.

"Jihoon, food doesn't just nourish you. It affects a person in an incomparable way," his mother once said to him. "The experience of taste, there's a whole world there. It changes people, it makes them whole."

Jihoon has never forgotten that lesson. Because every cell of his body missed his mother's cooking when she died. He would stay in the kitchen late at night, after closing time, dousing his throat with shots of soju while trying to recreate his mother's kimchi jjigae, bulgogi deopbap, sundubu jjigae, and ramen. None of it ever came close. Perhaps it was a fool's errand, trying to drum up tastes from the past, because a mother's cooking is never replicable, or so Koreans typically say.

He throws away the half-spent cigarette into the street and goes back inside. He checks on his lone customer, who seems to have finished a third of her soju bottle. From behind the counter, he pulls out his old copy of *The Golden Compass*, which he would read in his mother's restaurant during breaks. One corner of the cover has been torn away, leaving a small beige triangle. The bottom right edge of the book is all curled up, and he sees the many dog ears where he marked the last page he read. He has read it dozens of times now and he knows what happens intimately, but he revisits it again and again. The same places, the same characters, the same stories.

•

In the days after his mother's funeral, there was so much to do. Jihoon decided that he did not want to keep the restaurant going, so it was sold to a small family whose five-year-old looked ecstatic at the prospect of his parents running a restaurant the size of a closet. For their one-room basement apartment, Jihoon told the landlord, an elderly man, that his mother had gone back to the countryside to join her family and he would be getting a room close to where he would go to university.

There was the savings account that his mother had left. At the bank the teller showed Jihoon how much his mother had accumulated over the years. He remembered all her old jackets, which she would wear even when some of the buttons fell off. She owned so very little clothing that he could count on one hand the number of outfits she would wear. She never wore makeup and never bought any beauty products. All those pennies she had pinched had gone into this savings account, earmarked for his tuition.

The most difficult part was when he discovered that his mother had registered for life insurance some years back.

When the payout came through, he wanted to rip the cheque into pieces. Even though the money clearly outlined the worth of his mother, he also knew that it had to be used with the greatest consideration. It was money that he had received in exchange for his mother's life, and it needed to be spent in a meaningful way.

It turned out that Jihoon aced his Suneung. As the cream of the crop of the nation's students, he would be able to go to Seoul National University. When he graduates he would have his pick of companies to work at. He would be given the world. But he has no intention to go to Seoul National, let alone any of the other top schools. He wants to leave.

After distracting himself with mandatory army service for the next two years, he decides to go to Europe. He is going to travel and see all the places that he was supposed to see with his mother. In Europe he wanders aimlessly for a few weeks. The money is not lacking, and he has all the time in the world. There is no one to be beholden to and there is nothing to go after. There are no more tests to write and no more goals to achieve. He walks around Paris, trying to see all the places that his mother had wanted to go to, like Notre Dame, but it doesn't give him any pleasure. He flies across the channel to London, not because he particularly wants to go but because he has nowhere else to go.

The idea to go to Oxford comes when he passes a bus stop near Victoria station and sees the words "Oxford Tube." He is reminded of the legendary university he has read about, the setting of his favourite book, and hops onto a double-decker bus. He tries to watch the scenery but falls asleep and is jolted awake when the bus rolls into Gloucester Green. He gets off and walks around, like he has done at all the other places. It's not clear where the famed university begins and ends. The city and the campus are tangled in symbiotic existence. He notices that Oxford is the same as everywhere else. The buildings, just as he expected, are old and grand. An air of refinement permeates through Oxford, which he does not care for.

As he gets farther away from the main campus, he sees more houses and shops and students walking about. He stops by a café and decides to sit down for a bit with a flat white; he takes out his ragged copy of *The Golden Compass*, which he starts reading for the fifth time on this trip. It was given to him by his mother. She'd been an avid reader of English literature before life got in the way, and this was the first book in English she had bought for Jihoon to share that part of her life with him.

Once he finishes a few dozen pages, he packs the book back in his bag and heads out into the street again. Not ten minutes into his walk, he comes across an abandoned Indian restaurant. He looks in through a large window and sees that the tables have started to collect layers of dust. There is a note on the door. The place is for sale and there is a number listed. He calls the number and hears that the former owner, an Indian man, has decided to move back to his home in Mumbai.

The next day, a realtor shows Jihoon the space and he can see potential. As he strolls around the kitchen in the back, barely lit by the afternoon sunshine coming through the front window, he imagines the smell of seolleongtang boiling to perfection, milky white and reminding him of the most comforting place on earth. He can see himself serving bulgogi jeongol on top of a portable gas range to an excited family of three. He can see himself finding a wife to run the restaurant with and a child who will help them just as he helped his own mother. He can see himself growing old in this place. He suddenly longs for a restaurant. A place of refuge for people seeking Korean food, just like from home. He wants people to raise their glasses here in celebration of friendship, family, and everything else, just as he had done with his mother. This is a good place. This could be a home.

 He returns to Korea and acts quickly to arrange the move. Everything is either thrown out or put in a container that will head over to the U.K. Before he departs, Jihoon decides to visit his mother's ashes in Sacheon one last time. He takes a coach bus from Seoul, then a taxi from the terminal to the mausoleum. Between him and his mother's urn is a square window. Right under it is her name, Pyo Yeongju. He asked a long time ago why his last name was not her last name, and she told him that it is customary to keep the father's last name for the child. When he said that he wanted to be Pyo Jihoon instead of Lim Jihoon, his mother gave him a bitter smile and said that she could not change what was already done.

 There is a white chrysanthemum laid next to the urn. He can't remember if he had left any flowers. He touches it. The petals are soft and fresh; someone has been here recently, perhaps an old friend of hers or even a stranger who had a flower left over and felt pity.

 Jihoon turns to leave and catch the bus to get back to Seoul. As he is about to step through the mausoleum's glass double doors, someone comes in and nearly bumps shoulders with him. Jihoon follows the man with his eyes, a gaunt middle-aged man with weathered skin, walking with a slight limp. He is wearing a black padded jumper and loose pants, and his grey hair is spotty across his scalp. The man stops in front of the window containing his mother's urn. He pulls out a chrysanthemum from the inside of his jacket and places it by the urn. He takes a moment and turns around. They make eye contact, and Jihoon can tell that the man knows him but is trying to hide it from him.

"Do you know her?" Jihoon asks.

"I do," the man says.

"So then you know me."

The man thrusts his hands in his pockets and looks to the side, visibly uncomfortable as he keeps his head down and fidgets in place. "No, I don't," he says, turning his face toward the ground.

"Would you have a drink with me?" Jihoon asks.

It is not desire but curiosity. With little to remember, he pictured his father from the way his mother described him. It always came out like a caricature of a terrible family patriarch from TV dramas who has a penchant for beating family members or like a tired alcoholic pouring soju into a glass and contemplating the twisted fate he has been put through. Now with his father in front of him, both versions seem so distant. He can't imagine that such a frail man used to slap his mother around until a tooth came flinging out.

His father accepts. They choose a place near the mausoleum, a hole-in-a-wall restaurant with few tables and a single server, not unlike the one that had been run by his mother. Jihoon orders some pork belly and a bottle of soju. As the meat sizzles and browns, they say nothing. His father quietly pours two shots for them.

"Let's geonbae," he offers. Jihoon accepts.

After the first drink, Jihoon grabs the bottle to pour this time. He does not want to give him the courtesy of using two hands, but he does anyway. The second shot goes down and

Jihoon feels looser with his emotions. "Were you really going to pretend you didn't see me back there?"

"I didn't want to bother you. Your mother made sure I never intruded on your life."

"I have your name. You've intruded plenty already."

The man does not answer.

"How did you even know it was me?"

"Your mother sent me letters with photos."

"What did she write?"

"How you were all doing. How much you've grown. How you were doing at school. That sort of thing."

His father reveals that after their departure, he continued to work on construction sites and spent his days soaked in soju. One day he slipped while carrying some materials up a slope, which led to an injury that left him permanently disabled. Now he works security at a local apartment building, which gives him a meagre wage and a small space to live in. He says it is cramped, but he feels it is more blessing than he deserves. He asks Jihoon what his plans are.

"I'm leaving," Jihoon says.

"For where?"

"Far. I'm leaving the country. I'm probably not going to come back. I never want to come back. I have to move and find a place of my own."

His father nods, like he understands, and asks no more questions after that. They empty the last bit of soju left in the bottle. It is their fourth and final. His father pays for the drinks and the food. Jihoon and his father shake hands, saying goodbye for what Jihoon considers is the last time. His father seems to linger, seemingly wanting something more, but Jihoon turns his back and walks away. He has no emotions left to express toward his father nor any sense of obligation as his son. He is as good as a stranger now.

The American

All her life, Yunah looked to her achievements as her guiding light. When her relationship with her church friends crumbled, she took flight to her exams. When her parents' marriage floundered, she let herself be blind to everything but her college applications. When she first experienced heartbreak, she could console herself with how her perfect GPA was opening doors unavailable to her classmates.

She walks along High Street, passing old storied buildings of knowledge, surrounded by young students walking up and down the street. There was a time when life was so simple. All she had to do was get good grades and be excellent. In fact, excellence was easy because there was a clear measure for it. It's partly why she never felt comfortable in the skin of Seonhye, who is a med school dropout. Yunah would never have dropped out of anything. How could Seonhye feel so comfortable, wandering about and living, marked by failure? That's not who Yunah is.

As she gets close to the Soju Club, she sees the owner outside, having a smoke. He waves to her. "Seonhye," he calls out.

She looks at the cigarette and feels a terrible hunger. She used to smoke in university to calm her nerves before exams. "You got another one there? Can I have one?"

"Of course."

Jihoon takes the pack from his pocket and passes her a cigarette. He then brings out the lighter. She leans in, lets the flame lick the tip as she takes a long drag followed by a trembling exhale. "Thanks," she says.

"No problem."

She looks Jihoon up and down while he is facing away. At first she observed him only from inside the car, parked across from the restaurant. She would watch Jihoon serve Doha and Junichi through the large windows in the front. After a while she had to check the place out. Not only because she needed to figure out how to get closer to them without being conspicuous but also because it looked suspicious. A Korean restaurant frequented by two North Koreans piqued her curiosity.

Yunah likes how clean the Soju Club always is. She couldn't stand how unkempt Korean restaurants used to look back on Long Island, the menu written in Korean on the wall in large old-fashioned font, posters of female celebrities advertising soju bottles, wallpaper peeling at the edges. This place has none of it. It is modern and relatively new. The owner is young, and he doesn't have the condescension that many older Koreans carry with them. He also speaks great English, which is a big plus since she always felt unsure about her Korean.

As they stand side by side, smoking, she feels like they have been friends, even though she has never exchanged any words with him beyond ordering from the menu. Her father used to tell her that Koreans naturally flock to one another wherever they go. She used to scoff at this as silly nostalgia-driven bias. Why would anyone leave Korea if they wanted to be around Koreans? She doesn't want to admit that her father is right. She thinks it's the fact that Jihoon looks just as stuck as she is in Oxford, waiting for it to end one way or another.

"You're quite young to run a restaurant. How old are you, exactly?" she asks.

"Twenty-five. That's not that young."

"You're younger than me. So you graduated school and your family just let you set up a restaurant all the way out in Oxford?"

"Something like that."

"Why?"

"Because I wanted to do it."

"But why here?"

"Why not here?"

It sounds unthinkable to make such big decisions on a whim, just because he wanted to. She thinks there must be something more, but it is not impossible. Her parents made such a move before she was born. "I'm just saying, you could've gone anywhere. Why here? It would've been better for business if you went to London, Manchester, or Liverpool."

"My favourite childhood book was *The Golden Compass*. It starts off in Oxford," Jihoon says. "Maybe that's why. Got in my head somehow. It's a pretty city. I like the buildings."

"I got sick of it in weeks," Yunah admitted.

"Yeah, I get it. But it's not like I stayed for the buildings."

"So why stay?"

Jihoon thinks for a moment, draws on his smoke longer than usual, and exhales deeply.

"I don't want to go back. And if I don't want to go back, I have to choose a place to live, right? I'm already here."

Jihoon's cigarette burns close to his fingers. He puts it out. Yunah, too, has reached the end.

"Can I have another one?" she asks.

"Here, keep the pack. You're coming in, right? To eat?"

She nods with a smile and lights another cigarette as Jihoon goes inside. Alone, she feels the nicotine rush to her head and looks up at the darkening sky, turning the day into the evening.

Her head feels light. It feels like she could float up there, leave all this behind. She finally understands why her father used to step out for walks by himself, sneaking a pack of smokes when her mother wasn't looking. The relief must have been sweet.

But in the end, he pushed on. It didn't matter what the world threw at him. So she will too. She will push on. She knows what she is doing.

CHAPTER 6

The Northerner

THE BLOND CHECKS HER PISTOL AND TUCKS IT BACK into her hip holster. She nods to the bearded one, who nods back. "CCTV showed a motorcycle pulling up to the place before it went down. So watch out for a black café racer," the bearded one says as she moves to the door.

"I'll be back shortly. We'll continue," the blond tells Yohan before she leaves. The certainty in her tone, that he would be here when she returned, amuses him. As if another possibility is unthinkable to her. Scenarios can infinitely diverge, and all he can trust is what he can see and hear. It is futile to try to place absolute conviction in anything that will happen in the future.

"There are people who plan for the future, and there are people who plan for the present," he recalls Dr. Ryu telling him. "Those who plan for the future rely on assumptions. They expect that there will be a tomorrow, a kind of tomorrow that fits into their projected narrative. It's why the powerful are obsessed with planning for the future. Only power can guarantee things. For us, however, we must plan in the present. We're not so lucky with our resources. We have to assume that we'll have nothing in the future."

Yohan had asked her what it meant, to plan in the present, and she had simply said, "To adapt, no matter what."

Yohan studies the lone American, left on his own to guard him. He is large, with thick, muscular arms, and his posture is relaxed even though his eyes remain vigilant. He sits down, looking at Yohan's many passports spilled all over the table. He picks one up, a Chinese one, and then moves onto another one, a Swiss one.

"It's impressive," the American says, putting down the last one he checks, a Russian one. "If I saw you on the street, I wouldn't think you're a North Korean. I suppose I've never seen one. You know, a real North Korean."

Yohan briefly glances at him and then turns to stare at the floor.

"How many people does it take to make one of you? How many trainees get squeezed into the system for someone like you to come out the other end?"

Yohan imagines how he could overtake him. He could leap up and put the man in a chokehold. That would require him to get very close, though, and Yohan is doubtful whether the bearded man would afford him the distance.

"I read that in some parts of your special forces, trainees go through a death match. Did you have to do that? Did you have to kill a friend to get here? Maybe several?"

Or it could be a swift kick to the temple, but the motion would be too wide, and it would give the opponent plenty of time to react.

"C'mon, we're gonna be waiting for a bit. I just want to talk to you. Get to know you. Maybe I can help you understand why going with us would be the better way."

Just as Yohan is about to tell him to shut his mouth, there is a faint creak upstairs. The American has noticed it as well. He takes a pair of plastic cuffs from his pocket and ties Yohan's hands in the front. The American seems calm but makes a rookie mistake: he does not notice that Yohan presents his hands with his thumbs touching and fists facing downward.

"Stay here," the American says, then pulls out his side arm. Slowly, he approaches the door to the staircase, opens it, and then closes it behind him.

After the American is out of sight, Yohan turns his hands inward so they are touching. He unclenches them, which affords him slack in the cuffs, and shimmies out of them. With his ears carefully tuned to the sounds above, Yohan hears a thud and a series of stomps. There is a fall and the sound of various objects crashing to the floor. He hears a muffled grunt and a loud thump followed by a series of groans, as if one of them is getting repeatedly hit. It all stops at some point. He hears footsteps coming down the stairs. The door opens. It is not the bearded American. Instead it is the employee from the Soju Club. Deoksu with his long hair tied in a neat ponytail.

"Kim Yohan-ssi," Deoksu says in a light, formal tone. It is as if he is still using his serving voice from the Soju Club, polite and patient.

Yohan's brows twitch at the mention of his real name. Deoksu nods with a satisfactory grin. Yohan recalls all the times he and Doha had stopped by the Soju Club. He remembers little of Deoksu because he was mostly in the kitchen. The few times he served dishes and poured water, he never said a word to anyone.

The Southerners could afford to be bolder than the Northerners. Unlike them, the Southerners could go about their business in the light of the world, and they didn't have to disguise themselves. They did not have to launder their identities to a point of forgetting who they were, which meant that they would leave a trail for others to follow. But there were no such traces for Deoksu and Jihoon. Every node of information checked out.

So Deoksu is a surprise. There was no other name assigned to his face or his likeness, and nothing warranted further research. Yet here he is, a secret watcher without any connection. Deoksu is as fictional as Junichi. It is likely not even his actual name.

"I thought you and the Americans were allies," Yohan says back in Korean.

"Not for everything and certainly not for this," Deoksu says.

Yohan stares down Deoksu. He can see Deoksu's calm facade being punctured by anxiety. Deoksu pulls out a pistol and lets it hover around his hip but does not point it at Yohan. "I've waited five years for one order to come down, so I'm not going to have any qualms about what I have to do to get what I need. Where are you meeting Dr. Ryu?"

"Is Jihoon also in on this?"

"Jihoon is just a helpful citizen."

"Does he know that he's involved?"

"What does it matter? Nothing will happen to him."

Yohan looks Deoksu up and down. He realizes they are of the same breed, the kind that follows orders.

"Location," Deoksu says.

"Thornhill Park and Ride," Yohan says without hesitation. If the Americans are guilty of an overabundance of confidence, the South Koreans emanate a cold efficiency that comes from their history of losses. They, like the North Koreans, have learned the lesson that the meek must strike decisively and ruthlessly when an opportunity arises. For that reason, Deoksu is a real threat. Yohan wants to keep him as far away from Dr. Ryu as possible. Thornhill Park and Ride is a believable meetup point, but it's also a safe distance from the Soju Club.

"After you, then," Deoksu says, withdrawing his firearm and lifting his hand toward the door.

Yohan quietly gathers his many passports and documents from the table and puts them all into his empty backpack. Outside the pub, a black Volkswagen Golf with a driver at the wheel and the engine running waits at the curb. The driver, bald and heavy-set, exchanges a look with Deoksu as he opens the back door. Yohan gets in, and Deoksu goes around to get in the passenger seat.

"What time are you supposed to meet?" Deoksu asks.

"Soon."

"When is soon?"

"I don't know. I was only given a location."

Deoksu whispers something to the driver. He turns his head around. "If she doesn't show up before midnight, I'm putting a bullet through your head. So if you're lying, you should tell us now."

"That's all I know."

"Where's the plane?" the driver asks Deoksu.

"Abingdon," Deoksu answers, glancing back at Yohan as if he is wary of revealing this piece of information to him.

Yohan maps out his next course of action. He could improvise an escape and slip away, put a bit of buffer between him and the South Koreans. Just enough to not have them hot on his tail. He looks around. The neighbourhood they are passing through is quiet. The hour is late, and the city is known for sleeping early. The streetlights are dimly lit, barely enough to illuminate the road. No cars are coming from the other side.

A café racer suddenly enters the lane in front of the car from a three-way intersection, which prompts the driver to hit the brakes. The three men in the car all jerk forward. Yohan barely manages to keep himself from hitting his nose on the back of the headrest.

"Ay-ssyang, what was that?" the driver cries.

The motorcyclist turns his torso and fires a suppressed pistol into the windshield. The bullets first strike the driver, who is instantly killed. The driver's hold on the brakes loosens, and the car starts slowly rolling forward as more rounds hit the front and go through the rear window. Yohan crouches as much as he can in the backseat. Deoksu pulls out his pistol, opens the door, and uses it as a cover to peer out the window. A bullet shatters it and shards spill over him.

Yohan opens the door and gets out of the car. He inches forward, trying to keep up with the vehicle as it rolls down the road. On the other side, he can see Deoksu shooting back. Yohan moves to the rear of the car and crouches down. Deoksu is completely distracted, occupied by the unknown threat at the front. Yohan looks sideways and sees a narrow street between tightly packed houses just a few metres away from him. This is his chance, and he takes it.

The air hisses around him and rounds snap at the asphalt near his feet as he springs up from cover and sprints toward the street. He vaguely hears Deoksu calling after him, but he looks back and sees no one chasing him. Yohan runs through the city streets, hurriedly turning corners and checking every now and then to see whether anyone is following. Every time a set of headlights passes by, he crouches down behind parked vehicles on the side of the road. When he is sure that he is a good distance away, he slows to a brisk walk. He then heads south, drawing the directions in his head.

Soju Club, Dr. Ryu.

He needs to get on Cowley Road. He avoids the main street and begins to make his way through tight passages. Just as he is running down an alleyway paved with cobblestones, he sees a motorcycle speed past the end of the alley and screech to a complete stop. The rider rolls the bike back into Yohan's view. It is the same café racer who just ambushed them. Yohan freezes, waiting for the attacker to raise his pistol at him. There is nowhere to go.

Yohan hears muffled Korean through the helmet. "Don't be alarmed, dongmu. I'm here under Dr. Ryu's orders. Come with me."

Yohan is hesitant, but the man takes his helmet off and shows his face. It is the comrade who died in Bergen.

•

Yohan wakes up from his short nap when a knock sounds on his door. He kicks his legs out of bed, alert, ready to fight or run, even in his own home. He hears a familiar voice.

"It's me. I've got news," Doha says.

Yohan opens the door and sees Doha grinning, holding up a green bottle with the red cursive Chinese letters of the Ryongseong label. Yohan guesses that Doha has good news since a bottle of Ryongseong is often brought out to celebrate.

Yohan's apartment in Pyongyang is small. A room with unpainted concrete walls, a modest kitchen, and a tiny bathroom the size of a closet. For someone his age, this is luxury. Yohan grabs a table propped up against the wall, unfolds the legs, and puts it on the ground. They sit across from each other, cross-legged on the floor. Yohan gets up to fetch two cups, but Doha signals him to settle back down. "I've brought my own glasses. You don't drink Ryongseong in a plastic cup." He takes out two small crystal glasses, ideal for a good shot of soju.

Yohan moves to take the bottle and pour, but Doha again stops him. He grabs the bottle, twists the brown metal cap open, and generously fills the two glasses. Yohan takes his glass with two hands and meets Doha's glass in the middle. They raise their drinks up to their lips and empty the shot into their throat with a sharp flick of their wrists. Yohan frowns as the alcohol burns down his neck.

"Congratulations." Doha breathes in through his teeth, feeling the soju rubbing away at his insides.

"What for?"

"You've made it. You're getting out of here."

Doha had told Yohan numerous times that he was preparing Yohan toward an opportunity to join foreign intelligence. For all the years he had studied, trained, and endured, this was his North Star, placed in his sky by his mentors. Yohan was expecting it, but he is relieved to hear the news. Finally, he has fulfilled what Doha and Dr. Ryu wanted for him all this time.

"I told you," Doha smiles. "You're the perfect candidate. I knew it. Hongjin knew it."

"Where is Dr. Ryu?" Yohan asks.

"Busy preparing. A lot of groundwork to do before the team is sent off. Paperwork up to the neck."

Yohan wishes she was here to congratulate him as well. He recalls the days when Dr. Ryu would spend the evenings teaching him foreign languages. He never knew what they were for, but he knew that if he memorized the proper vocabulary, Dr. Ryu would smile at him, give him a pat on the back, and tell him that he was doing well.

Yohan accepts another shot from Doha. "Where will we be going?"

"First to Vladivostok. From there, we'll get on a cargo ship. The ship will make its way to Italy, where we will stop at our embassy and be given our assignments."

"Sounds far."

"It is very far."

The first time he saw Europe on a map was when Dr. Ryu was giving him a geography lesson. The education available at the orphanage had been miserable at best, so Dr. Ryu had to tutor him, make sure he was caught up in order to enroll him in school. He remembers how small North Korea seemed compared to the rest of the world and how close his enemies, the South, were. And how far the devilish American imperialists were, all the way across the ocean.

"Does this mean I'll never come back?"

"Here?"

"Yes, the motherland."

He notices a tinge of surprise in Doha's eyes. Yohan knows he should be grateful for this special assignment. Yohan always had a clearer sense of what he needed to do, thanks to Doha and Dr. Ryu.

"Why?" Doha asks.

Yohan stumbles on his words. He looks away from Doha, focusing on the empty shot glass he keeps turning in his fingers.

"Are you nervous? Scared?"

Yohan shakes his head. There is nothing that scares him. If he were told to go assassinate the South Korean president, no matter how impossible it may be, he would do it without hesitation.

"Yohan, a lot of things will change, but don't drown in uncertainty, because it becomes a weight that you can't cast off. And by the time you realize that you must make a decision, it's too late."

They drink together, and Doha pours another. "I've done many things that should have destroyed me. I've sent men to Yodok. Men with families, men who served the republic with everything they had. Good men, loyal men. Men who didn't deserve such things to happen to them. But I did it to survive. It was the only way to stay away, to be free from this place. So get out and do your best. Make yourself useful and don't look back."

A rumble sounds outside as a convoy of trucks passes by the apartment complex. Yohan glances at the window as the sound of the convoy disappears into the distance. Doha looks at the bottle and sees that it is empty. A hiccup lifts his shoulders. "It is a strange place out there, Yohan. You will struggle to adapt, but you cannot afford to make a mistake. You'll have to do exactly as I say. Keep every word from me and Dr. Ryu sacred. Follow every instruction. Will you do that for me?"

"I will."

"Good." Doha grins. "I'm proud of you. I've seen a lot of talented boys come and go, but you've easily outshined all of them. We set a high bar for you, and you leapt over it masterfully. I'm proud of all that you have done," Doha tells him. Yohan can only nod in response. "Forget this place. Forget it all. If we're lucky, we'll never come back here. This wretched land."

Yohan does not understand this animosity toward their home, but he accepts it because it is Doha. If Doha says it, it must be true. Perhaps it's a way for Yohan to commit to the mission. To feel no attachment so he can truly start his life and make a new home.

They raise their glasses for the final time that night. It is the last drink he will ever have in his home country.

The Southerner

Jihoon takes stock for the next day. He counts how many ingredients he has and examines how much banchan he'll have to make for tomorrow, such as namul, blanched soybean sprouts, or those sweet boiled potatoes that Deoksu excels at.

He notices the garbage is overflowing and realizes he hasn't had proper time to clean up. The kitchen is a mess. He ties up the garbage bag and heads out to the dumpster. When he opens the back door, he sees Deoksu standing there, as if he was just about to open the door as well.

"Deoksu-ya. What are you doing in the back alley?"

"I just want to come in," Deoksu says hurriedly. There is something in his tone that unnerves Jihoon slightly. For all the time he has known Deoksu, he has never seen him in a rush.

"Sure, but through the back?"

"I thought this would be more discreet. I just need to get something from the kitchen."

"Discreet? You work here, Deoksu-ya."

"I don't want to disturb the customers."

"There's only one person in there. Just a lady."

"A lady? By herself?" Deoksu's eyes light up at the mention of this for some reason. "What does she look like?"

"Well, she's an ajumma, except she looks very refined. Good taste in clothes, short hair. I don't know, I wasn't looking that closely."

"Is she Korean?"

"She spoke in English, so I'm not sure. She could be."

"She could be," Deoksu mumbles.

"Are you expecting someone?" Jihoon asks.

"No, nothing like that. I have a friend in town and he's here with his mother. I'm just wondering if that's her."

"You have a friend? Where is he now? Tell him to come to the restaurant."

"No, it's okay. He's out right now and I'm joining him later. Here, I'll take the garbage out for you."

"Oh, thanks." Jihoon hands Deoksu the garbage bag for the short trek from the back door to the dumpster.

While in the kitchen, Jihoon hears the back door opening and closing and looks up to see Deoksu in the doorway, leaning out and checking the dining hall.

"Is it her? Your friend's mother?" Jihoon asks.

"Can't tell. Probably not."

There is a ding at the entrance, announcing a new guest. Deoksu snaps his head back, as if he is trying to hide. Jihoon peers through the kitchen window and smiles upon seeing Seonhye.

"I'll take this," Deoksu quickly says. He briskly steps out into the hall and guides Seonhye to a table, one close to where the lone woman is sitting. This startles Jihoon. Deoksu has never volunteered to take an order from a customer. Usually, he keeps to himself, and Jihoon never sees him outside work hours. He feels like he has stumbled upon a side of Deoksu he has yet to discover until now.

Jihoon watches Deoksu take an order from Seonhye. She usually doesn't bother looking at the menu. Kimchi jjigae is her go-to. Deoksu keeps glancing at the other occupied table, presumably to see if the woman is his friend's mother or to see whether she needs anything.

Jihoon suddenly thinks about asking Deoksu to take over the dining hall next week. It would be accompanied with a raise. Not that he expects that would convince Deoksu to stay. He then could have more time to think about making improvements to the place. The space needs some change. Since he opened, he has never adjusted the menu, and he wants to add a new ramen. That would be just the start. There are so many other dishes he wants to try. Ones that were never on his mother's menu. He feels ready to move beyond it. After Deoksu leaves to go back to Korea, perhaps he'll close for a few weeks, even a month, to catch his breath and make this place more whole. For the first time in a long while after his mother's departure from the world, Jihoon feels a sensation akin to waking up from a deep sleep.

•

When Jihoon returns to Oxford, he feels at ease. He takes short trips to London in order to visit Korean restaurants for inspiration. He notices how cramped the subway is compared to Seoul. He watches the oddly shaped taxis bump along the wrong side of the road, and he reminds himself that over here, the other side is the right side.

The restaurant is due to open in a month. He has been cooking alone in the kitchen for weeks to figure out the menu. He has never really done everything by himself or made anything from scratch. His mother was always there with the broth already prepared or the sauce ready-made. And she didn't leave written recipes. Everything was always done by eyeing or tasting for the right amount of salt and heartiness.

It takes a few days to get the seasoning just right for the sundubu so that it tastes close to the one his mother made. He does the same with budae jjigae, seolleongtang, and bulgogi jeongol. One by one, he fills the menu. Each dish gives hints to the next and consolidates his memory of his mother's cooking.

On the day he masters the last item on the menu, gamja-tang, he goes outside and takes out one of the last items of his mother's he has kept — the pack of cigarettes she had in her possession when she was hit by the car. He had never smoked in his life, but his mother often did. Holding his mother's favourite brand of cigarettes, THIS, he lights one up in remembrance of her and closes his eyes, imagining that she is congratulating him, smoking with him. It reminds him of those rituals they do back in Korea, where they splash a grave with soju and consider it sharing a drink with the dead.

"Excuse me?"

He opens his eyes, expecting an Englishman, but instead he finds a middle-aged Asian man. His hair is greying here and there, and webs of wrinkles are starting to spread from the edges of his eyes.

"Are you the owner?"

"Yes, I am."

"There used to be an Indian restaurant here."

"They closed. I bought the place. I'm turning it into a Korean restaurant."

The man peers through a window of the restaurant while Jihoon burns through the cigarette. He steps backward, takes in the whole view of the restaurant, and looks at Jihoon. "I knew the owner. I used to come here a lot back when I was a student. I have a lot of good memories of this place."

Jihoon throws the stub to the ground, smudges it with the tip of his shoe, and asks, "Would you like to come in?"

"Oh no, I don't want to intrude."

"No, I wasn't doing anything in particular. How about a drink? It's not much to look at inside, but if you don't mind."

"I never say no to a drink." He smiles.

In the empty restaurant, Jihoon unfolds the legs of a plastic table he had brought in as a makeshift eating spot and snaps open two portable chairs. "All I've got so far is soju. Would that be okay with you?"

"Yes, soju would indeed be nice."

He brings out two shot glasses and a green bottle of soju from the fridge that he had ordered from Korea. The first few drinks they share in silence. The man is relaxed and chatty, reminiscing about his student days in Oxford and how he could never find anyone to befriend then. He talks about his first love, whom he met at the university. They were happy together, but they went their separate ways after graduation. They both got jobs and lived in different cities until they were reunited through work.

"What happened afterwards?"

"By that time, she had a child with her. I was happy to be with her, and as long as the child was hers, I was ready to love him and be his father."

Jihoon looks at how his face brightens when the child is mentioned. He finds himself smiling along with the man.

"Growing up, my own father was never in the picture. He was there financially. My mother and I had a nice apartment, a car with a driver, a housemaid, and all the money we ever needed. I truly thought that was what fatherhood was for a long time. You take care of them by providing. Now I realize how deprived I was," he says this with a laugh and drinks.

Jihoon follows and refills their glasses. "Right," he nods in agreement.

Jihoon wonders if this is the moment where he opens up about his own father, though the man doesn't ask. He can perhaps talk about it, but it is pointless. The experience is not of loss, because he doesn't remember a life in which he had a father. So he keeps it hidden away in a corner where he does not have to think about it too often. All he ever had was his mother.

When the bottle is empty, the man stands up and nods in gratitude. "This was lovely. Thank you."

Jihoon also stands up. They shake hands.

"Does this place have a name? I'd like to come back when you open."

"Not yet."

"May I suggest one?"

"Sure."

"How about the Soju Club?"

"Soju Club?"

"It's a place for soju."

"But it's not just a place for soju," Jihoon chuckles.

"Of course it's not, but it's a place for people to have soju and enjoy each other's company. Like we just did."

"I'll consider it," Jihoon says.

The American

The kimchi jjigae arrives along with a bowl of fresh rice, just as she has enjoyed for the past two years while in Oxford. She takes a breath, readying herself before what could be her last meal of the mission. The jjigae is still boiling in the black stone pot. She inhales the aroma along with the steam.

The first time she ever had kimchi jjigae was with her grandmother. She flew in from Samcheonpo all the way to Long Island to take care of little Yunah since her parents were always working — at the time, her father was an educational CD salesman for a man he had met at church; her mother tutored math for kids of parents she had also met at church. This was the best they could do with the credentials they brought from Korea. For a long while, her grandmother did all the household chores and raised Yunah while her parents worked and saved money.

Her grandmother would do these grand gimjang days every now and then and make a batch of kimchi out of twenty cabbages. Yunah's mother complained that it took up all the room in the fridge, but her grandmother ignored these protests because they all knew that there was no alternative. When the kimchi soured, kimchi jjigae made the rounds on the table for weeks. When her grandmother finally left — as Yunah entered high school — kimchi practically disappeared from the house because no one bothered to make it. It was in Oxford, after over a decade since her grandmother's departure, that she had tasted kimchi jjigae again.

Right as Yunah is about to take a spoonful of the boiling soup, someone enters the restaurant. She looks up and sees the blond, her face matching that of the faxed dossier. She waves at her as if they are friends. Without asking for permission, the blond pulls out a chair and sits. "Choi."

Yunah doesn't bother to answer. She takes her first spoonful and the flavours hit right away, leaving her to savour the sensation of the hot saltiness spreading deep down into her gut. The heat overwhelms her. She opens her mouth and pants.

"Why don't you wait until it's cooled?" the blond asks.

"It's not the same. You have to eat it when it's boiling hot."

The blond responds only by shaking her head. Yunah continues to eat.

"I told you to stay at the hospital," the blond says.

"I'm aware," Yunah says in between scooping rice into her mouth.

"Care to explain?"

"I was hungry."

"You were hungry, so you disobeyed."

"Sure, let's say that."

The blond scoffs. "So this attacker shot Manning, and you just fought the guy off without even a weapon?"

Yunah swallows a pepper the wrong way and pauses, taking a napkin to her mouth and coughing. "Yes," she answers after her throat calms down.

"See, something doesn't track. There were three shots fired. One of them went into Manning, while two of them went into the wall near the door. They were shot, from what I could deduce, from the bathroom. Which means it wasn't a one-way attack. It was a shootout, yet Manning had the gun."

Yunah finally puts her utensils down and stares directly at the blond agent. She pulls the gun out and sets it down on the table, the barrel facing the blond. Yunah glances over at the lone Asian woman a few tables over from her and conceals the gun with a napkin.

"Where'd you get that?" the blond asks.

"I found it."

"You found a Glock 42 just lying around."

"It was hidden in the wall. In the bathroom."

"And how did you know that?"

"I was on the toilet for a long time."

"You sure it wasn't someone who told you that it was there?"

Yunah realizes the blond is hinting at treason. "Before you go about making up more bullshit, I'm going to make it clear. I know where my loyalties lie. I'm an American and American first."

"I never said anything about that," the blond says. "I just want to get the details of what happened."

"I have nothing else to say. What I said was what happened."

The blond leans in, a smirk spreading across her face as she does. "No, Agent Choi. What I say is what happened. Do you understand?"

Deoksu hurries over to them and Yunah quickly hides the gun back in her pants. Deoksu asks the blond if she wants anything. She waves him off, but Yunah asks for some more kimchi. He goes to the counter, shouts the order at Jihoon, and then checks in at the table with the lone woman.

The blond agent, who is sitting facing the windows, suddenly squints, looking past Yunah. Yunah turns around. A grey Volvo sedan has parked in front of the restaurant. The bearded agent makes his way to the entrance, where he forcefully swings the door open. He is furious and seems to be looking for someone. Deoksu's hand goes to his hip to pull out his handgun while the bearded agent's hand reaches inside his jacket to reveal a suppressed pistol, and they end up in a standoff.

From the kitchen Jihoon peers out with a plate of kimchi. "Deoksu-ya, here's the kimchi she asked for."

This distracts Deoksu for a brief moment. The American rushes Deoksu and grabs his pistol. The gun goes off, and the bearded agent stumbles back and shoots three rounds. Deoksu bolts back to the kitchen as bullets chase him. The back door opens and shuts.

"Stop! Stop shooting!" the blond cries. Yunah hears a thud and sharply turns toward the kitchen, her gut sick with the realization of what just happened. She runs and finds Jihoon on the floor in the hallway, right next to the kitchen entrance, with two red blotches on his body, one in his stomach and another in his chest. A plate of kimchi lies spilled on the ground next to him, its sauce mingling with the blood pooling around his body.

"Holy shit," she says. "Holy shit, shit!"

She grabs an apron hanging on the wall, rolls it up, and presses it against Jihoon's chest wound. He is struggling to breathe, mumbling, "Eomma, Eomma," looking into her face with desperate eyes. She holds him until his words fade into silence.

CHAPTER 7

The Exiled

ON THE PLANE, I SQUIRM A BIT IN MY SEAT AND LOOK out the window. Doha laughs at my uneasiness and asks me if this is my first time. No, I have been on airplanes before. I was born into privilege. My mother was an actress and my father was a high-ranking general, just beneath that of the Great Leader in the military.

Doha chuckles again and goes back to his book. He always has a book with him. The first time I met him, he was sitting on a bench and reading *Dune* by Frank Herbert in English, right in the middle of the Kim Il Sung University campus, which was a capital offence. The unthinkable nature of this made me curious and I stopped in front of him. "Is that in English?"

He put the book down, revealing his face. His hair was short and his sleeves were rolled up. His jacket was thrown into a ball at his side, which gave me a sudden desire to carefully fold it. I did not know what shocked me more. The carelessness of his ensemble or his book.

"Yes."

"Where did you get it?"

"My mother," he said with a shrug.

"How did she get the book?"

He squinted as he examined me, trying to figure me out. "Listen, if you're from State Security, feel free to report me. I don't give a shit. But if you're not, here's the honest answer. I don't know. And I'm not interested in where it comes from. I only care that it's good reading material. All right?"

Before I could answer him, he went back to reading his book. No one could be this carefree in the face of potentially getting dragged in front of a firing squad. That is, unless their family had some serious pull with the regime.

"Who's your father?"

He sighed, dropping the book to his lap. "I don't have a father."

"What, you're a bastard, then?"

"I guess I am."

I was surprised because I said it as a joke, but he was calm and serious.

"You've never seen a bastard?"

"I just want to know where you got that book from."

"Do you want to read it? You can borrow it. I'm rereading it for the third time. Here, take it."

"What?"

"Take it. Read it and give it back to me when you're finished."

He pushed the book toward me. Admittedly, I was curious, but I backed away and looked around to see if this was a setup to weed out dissidents. Perhaps there was a hidden accomplice ready to spring out and witness this act of defiance against the republic. Or a photographer who would catch me red-handed with blasphemous reading material. It didn't take much evidence for anyone, even the highest-ranking officials, to end up in Aoji or Yodok and slowly die from hard labour.

"I'm not from State Security either, if that's what you're wondering."

I took the book. He walked away without another word, putting on his suit jacket, which looked boxy on him. Despite the ill-fitting suit, his casual gait and the way he put his hands in his pockets showed that he truly did not care whether anyone was watching. On campus, where everyone was under constant surveillance, such an attitude was not only puzzling but also admirable.

I returned the book to him after reading it. I read it all, from cover to cover, even though a science fiction novel about a ducal heir taking vengeance on a rival family of nobles was not something I was interested in.

"How was it?" he asked, sitting on the same bench as when I first saw him.

"It was good."

"That's all?" he scoffed. "You really don't have any other thoughts? What did you think of the main character?"

"Paul? Well," I said cautiously. "I liked him because he reminded me of the Leader."

He tipped his head, as if curious. "How?"

"Just like the character in the book, the Leader had to fight countless villains in order to bring peace and prosperity to the rest of us."

He stared at me. I saw his lips twitch into a grin for a moment. "What's the matter with you?" he asked. "You can't possibly think that this book reminded you of the Leader. Paul Atreides is a man who has everything but loses it all. The Leader does not know what loss means. Paul is someone who is aware of his own privilege and takes responsibility for it. The Leader has no such sense or awareness. And most importantly, Paul tries to find a way to reduce suffering and death. Do you honestly think the Leader does this?"

Before I could even express my shock at his flagrant insolence against the Leader, he started to walk away, his jacket hooked on his finger and draped over his back.

"Wait, wait," I said. "I'll tell you what I really thought."

He turned around and faced me. "All right, tell me, then."

"I didn't like it."

"Why?"

"It's all space and spice. I don't like any of it."

"But you said you read it all."

"Because you lent it to me."

"So you only read it all because you thought you had to, not because you wanted to?"

"Yes."

He chuckled, clicking his tongue. "You know, that's ridiculous. You don't owe me anything. Besides, I have other books you might like. Let me know if you want to read them."

Of course I wanted to read them all. At the time neither of us thought much of it. We were just bonding over books. But that was how it all started between us.

On the plane I open Ernest Hemingway's *A Farewell to Arms* and pick up from where I left off. Doha lent it to me after I expressed my enjoyment of *The Old Man and the Sea*.

We sit in silence, reading, until we land in Geneva. From there we take another flight to London and then a train to Oxford, where we will begin our education for the sake of the republic.

The Rejected

The blond flips the sign to "Closed." She checks in with headquarters, who assures her that no one has called the police about the gunshots.

"What was that for?" the blond says to the bearded man. "And why are you here?"

"I was attacked. He attacked me. Took me down and took the guy with him. I've been going everywhere trying to find him."

"You killed a man. He's a civilian," Yunah interrupts.

"You sure?" he asks.

"We did a background check. He was just a guy from Seoul who opened a restaurant here."

"What about the other guy?"

"He's an employee," Yunah says.

The bearded one seems to be thinking, looking down. "So he's one of theirs."

"One of whom? The North Koreans?"

"Think about it. If the guy who attacked me is an employee here, then this whole place is probably a North Korean cover. Just like the pub is our cover."

"No, that's not —"

"Watch her," the blond says to the bearded agent, pointing to the woman dining by herself, who seems to be minding her own business as if nothing out of the ordinary has occurred. She pulls Yunah to a quiet corner by the entrance. "Agent Choi, the story makes sense. After all, the North Koreans dined here regularly. That was in your reports."

"He wasn't attacking us. He's just a civilian."

"There are knives here; he could've attacked," the blond says. "And how do you explain that Doha and his dog were here so often? Maybe they were getting instructions. Through the menu perhaps? Kimchi jjigae, that could be a code."

"No, no!" Yunah cries out. "He's innocent. He has nothing to do with this. He's just some poor man who was trying his best to make a living out here. And you shot him in his own kitchen. Now you want to turn him into a criminal. I saw everything and I will not sign off on this! I won't!"

Yunah takes a step back, bracing for the impact of her outburst. The blond comes close, her face within millimetres of Yunah's. "Agent Choi, we will report all of this as we deem appropriate, and you will help us make the story fit. Those suspicions we have of you will stay as suspicions as long as you keep your mouth shut. Do you understand?"

Yunah realizes she is in no better position than Jihoon. At least he is dead. The blond acts quickly. "We widen the search, recover Mr. Nakamura, as well as this employee. Agent Choi, you watch this woman here. She's a witness to all this and a liability. We'll sort this out when we find them. Wait for us."

The blond woman and the bearded man exit and pile into the grey sedan parked outside, which jerks onto the road, prompting a honk from a passing car. Yunah walks over and sits across from the lone woman. "I'm sorry you have to deal with this. It won't be complicated. Just a few forms. You might even get compensation."

The woman's face is calm. So much so that Yunah is thrown off. It feels wrong for this woman, a witness to a man being killed with a gun, to be so poised. Yunah drops her arm by her side where she has her pistol.

"It's funny how they have it all wrong," the witness says, as if she has disregarded everything Yunah said. "The man who was just in here, he wasn't a North Korean. He's a South Korean. He has nothing to do with us, as you said. More importantly, we're not working together. Some enemies do, but we don't."

"Who are you?" Yunah asks.

The woman takes a sip of her drink. Her arm hangs on the back of her chair, her glass twirling slowly and idly in her fingers.

"I'm your seven p.m."

•

Yunah walks into the meeting room. There are two men at the table, and they ask her to take a seat.

"Hello there. Thanks for coming in. I'm Special Agent Nelson. This is Special Agent Cole. We're here to brief you on your next assignment."

Special Agent Cole continues. "Currently, we're tracking a North Korean spy cell across Europe, based out of Oxford. We've narrowed it down to a location, but we just can't get any specific intel or on-the-ground data. You'll be part of a small skeleton team that will set up a cover in the target area and report back on their activities."

"Now," Nelson says, "we do know the two people running it. First there is Doha Kim. This guy is basically their frontman. He doesn't hide. He operates completely in the open. He has a Ph.D. from Oxford, and he goes to all sorts of conferences and symposiums. The official word is that he's basically a PR op for the regime."

"Then there's the more elusive one, and his name is Dr. Ryu," Cole says. "This one is trickier because we know nothing about this individual beyond the fact that he's a high-ranking official in the regime. He has a doctorate in psychology and is responsible for recruiting, training, and handling agents."

"Is there a picture of this Dr. Ryu?" Yunah asks.

"No," Cole says.

"Then how do we know Dr. Ryu is a man?"

"Well, I mean, they always have been," Nelson says. "High up in the regime, allowed to leave the country. Gotta be a man."

"So if we don't know what he looks like, how do we even find him?" Yunah asks.

"We think Doha Kim meets with Dr. Ryu in Europe every three months. But that's all we have. We need more intelligence."

"What's the cover?"

"We're going to set up a bar," Cole says. "Or as they call it, a pub."

"Like a real pub? A full-on pub?"

"Yes."

For a while, they are all silent. Yunah does not know what to say. This is what all her training has come to, running a pub. "Why?"

"Our analysts have concluded that this is the most inconspicuous establishment we can set up."

"But why can't I just be a student at Oxford? I'll just watch from afar. Why the elaborate setup?"

They look at each other. Cole sifts through his papers and settles on a page. "This is just what we've been told. This is cleaner and easier. We rent the space using a shell company. You being a student leaves a trace in the system."

She is stunned that they don't think a pub won't leave a trace. But she knows the drill. This is not a time to argue. She needs to shut up, listen, and give acceptable answers. "What am I going to be doing, then?"

"Gathering information on the operatives of this spy cell."

"But the pub, the pub is a real pub, right? So are we hiring people to run it?"

"Uh, no outsiders for this mission. We're going to man this pub all on our own," Nelson says.

"Who's doing the work, then?"

"To be completely clear, you and one other team member," Cole says.

"I'm going to be serving drinks?"

"Yes," Nelson nods.

"Why?"

"It has to be real."

Yunah's head starts to hurt. "Okay fine, but are we serving food?"

"As far as we know, we are." Cole looks at Nelson, then answers. "Yes."

"That's impossible. I've worked at a bagel shop before, and I can tell you, this isn't going to work. There's no way we can keep an eye on anyone if it's just two people running a real pub."

"We've made the calculations," Nelson says. "It should work."

"Have you worked in a kitchen before?"

Neither of them answers. Of course they haven't. Nelson is from Yale, rowing team, his father a state senator. Cole played lacrosse and went to Stanford, his mother a biotech company executive.

"I'm just telling you; it's not going to work."

The two agents look at each other. "We'll circle back to this," Cole says.

"You are Korean, yes?" Nelson continues after flipping through a few more papers.

"My parents are Korean."

"So you're Korean."

"Yes, but I was born here."

"No, what we mean is that ethnically, you are Korean."

"Yes. Do you need me to speak Korean?"

"No, that's not necessary. These people don't even pose as Koreans when they're in the field, so English is fine. All we want is for them to just take some interest in you. We want you to make friends with them." Nelson clears his throat and continues. "Once they do take interest in you, the mission will be to extract information out of them. Get them to talk. Give them more booze. Make them spill as many details as possible."

"So you want me to be doing all of this as a bartender?"

"Yes, you're going to be …" Cole looks down at his papers and recites the information back at Yunah, "… a South Korean medical school dropout working as a bartender in Oxford. That's your cover."

"Why a dropout?"

"It fits, doesn't it? Drops out of med school to explore the world."

It doesn't make sense to her. She would have finished what she had started and explored the world afterward. She already feels so distant from her alias.

"Okay, whatever, but I just told you I speak very little Korean. I understand a bit, but that's it."

"No, all you need to do is to put up a facade that you are Korean, just enough to get them to talk to you. We don't want any Korean spoken. We've tried that, and they've always gotten suspicious. They're far too careful."

"Try to throw in an accent though," Nelson adds. "Just to make it believable."

"Believable that I'm a South Korean?"

"Precisely. Gotta give some effort to make it authentic, right? Don't worry, we have a coach for that."

Logistics are discussed and it is settled that Yunah will fly out the following week. She shakes both of their hands and walks out of the office, buttoning up her suit jacket. She walks back to her own office, a small windowless room in the corner of her division. When she closes the door and sits on her chair, she lets herself feel optimistic despite her discomforts. This is a stepping stone at least. If she succeeds, she will be able to escape this room and go elsewhere. This could be an opportunity. That is, as long as she does as she is told.

The Nameless

Yohan and the comrade arrive at a three-storey residential building on the outskirts of the city. The comrade's apartment is dimly lit, with a small rectangular window. It's furnished with a single bed, a couch, a table, and two chairs. There is a small kitchen and a bathroom.

The comrade takes off his helmet and puts on a kettle to boil.

"How are you alive?" Yohan asks. "I saw you die. In Bergen."

"Oh," the man says, then slowly sits down at the table. Yohan joins him. "The last thing I saw was your face. It went black, but then I woke up and there were people from the

Bureau. I thought I was in hell. Surely it couldn't be heaven if I was still being hounded by the Bureau. They brought me back. They were probably waiting right outside. You might've even passed their car when you left."

Yohan does not remember anything of the kind.

"I didn't know who they were. They were probably the New Leader's men. They offered the same thing — I'd be rewarded handsomely back home and they would take care of my omani. They wanted me to spy on you. Now here I am."

"Was it you, then? Did you kill him?"

"Who? Oh, the commander. No, that was not me."

"Do you know who did it?"

"I only know what I've been told, dongmu."

Yohan looks down to collect his thoughts, then asks, "Did Dr. Ryu say anything about what to do with me?"

"You?" the comrade says as he laughs. "Her exact instructions were to ensure that you are safe. To eliminate all obstacles in your path. And to make sure no one captures you."

"What happens now?"

"Well, you're going to take the motorcycle and get out of here. Get out of this city."

"To where?"

"Anywhere. Go anywhere you want."

"That's not an answer. I can't just go anywhere. She must've given a destination."

"She didn't. She told me to just let you go, let you get out of here."

The kettle whistles, and the comrade gets up to make tea. He gestures with his head toward the kettle to see if Yohan wants any. He declines. It doesn't make sense to him that Dr. Ryu would say this. The command has no objective and is completely open ended. There are no parameters, no variables. In fact, the potential outcomes are infinite.

"You're with the Bureau, yet this isn't what they would order. Why let me go?" Yohan asks.

"Dr. Ryu said so."

"But this is insubordination."

The comrade gives this a thought. "I suppose."

"What is this?" Yohan says. "What is really happening?"

The comrade laughs. "You think the Leader is watching us now while we commit this act of betrayal? I know what they say, what we learned. The Leader is all-seeing and everywhere. He sees when you take your morning coffee. He scorns you when you use a phone made by capitalist pigs. He hears when your piss hits the toilet water. But for all of that, what happens in the end?"

The comrade laughs again. "I mean look at the two of us. You got an order to kill me. Now I have an order to kill you. It's just us out here, being told to kill each other in the name of whom? The Leader? He doesn't care. Not about me or my omani." The comrade's voice cracks. He takes a deep breath to compose himself.

"Dr. Ryu told me that my omani is dead. She said that she was taken out and executed the very day I was deployed. She even proved it to me. Showed me the document that had Doha dongji's signature on it. Showed me documents for every operative who had to leave the republic, their families shot dead and buried. All except you. You didn't have a single document to your name."

Yohan recalls the files Doha showed him as they were disposing of their records in their final days together in Oxford. It was all in a black binder that chronicled the fate of the operatives' family members. It was to keep them in the dark and to make sure the operatives never returned to the republic. They were tainted goods, treated as if they were covered by the disease of foreign influence, and their destinies were sealed once they left the borders of North Korea.

"Back then, it didn't make sense to me really. You being an orphan. You've got no one back home. I thought that meant that you could have defected any time. But I realized that it was the opposite. You have nothing to miss, nothing to remember. During nights, you don't recall how comfortable your omani's embrace used to be. You're the fortunate one, dongmu. Free from the bounds of hyo."

The word "hyo" echoes in Yohan's mind. He has never considered it a freedom. He would watch others and wonder what hyo would feel like. The loyalty a child has for a parent, a luxury that he will never know because his mother and father abandoned him. Before he could have a chance to give his loyalty to family, they were gone from his life and left him to be watched over by a bitter old orphan master, a war hero who won medals just to be condemned to take care of little runts who could barely lift a shovel.

But he has known Doha and Dr. Ryu. Comrades came and went, but Doha and Dr. Ryu were the two pillars in his life. They not only taught him how to perform his duty as a son of the republic, but also to see the world from different perspectives. Memories flood into him. An introduction to Shostakovich by Doha, who explained the background of each piece as the record player boomed in their apartment. An invitation to a gallery in London, where Dr. Ryu asked for his thoughts on abstract paintings. A discussion around a novel recommended by Doha, in which Yohan struggled to say anything of substance. There was also an evening stroll and quiet chat in Amsterdam with Dr. Ryu holding his arm and asking him if he could envision a different life. He hadn't known what to say. Nothing had come to his mind then.

"Be patient with yourself. You will know in time what to do," she had said to him. "You are more than simply the service you provide."

"Do you think I'll ever know it?" Yohan asks the comrade. "Hyo?"

"You can't," the comrade smirks as he sips his tea. "Hyo is loyalty toward those who raised you. Nobody raised you."

"I see."

"Trust me," the comrade says. "You don't want it. Hyo. The burden of duty to the one who gave birth to you, who fed you, clothed you, made you whole. Especially when you can't do anything about it. Every night after I was brought back to life, I'd dream of my mother. I would cry out and she would just stand there, silent. I'd sometimes go for several nights without sleeping because of those dreams. But now I get to rest. I can finally join her and fulfill my duty as a son."

The comrade hangs his head in fatigue. He goes to his desk and pulls out a drawer. He takes out a small metal box with a pill, just like the one Yohan had given him in Bergen. "This one's supposed to be real," he smiles bitterly as he holds it up.

Without any delay or a thought afterward, he pops the pill into his mouth and promptly swallows it with the last gulp of his tea. He lies down on the bed, closes his eyes, and waits. "You can go now," he says. "The bike key is in my jacket."

A brief silence passes and Yohan blurts out, "You don't have to die. You can also try to run."

The comrade lifts his head up just enough to see Yohan. "Dongmu, I have nothing I want to live for in this world. Once Dr. Ryu told me the truth, that was it. It was all undone. My loyalty, everything. I may not have anything to live for because my earthly connections have all been severed, but that doesn't mean the same for you. You can go anywhere, be anyone. It's freedom."

"I don't even know if I want this. I never asked for it."

"And I never asked to be brought back, yet here I am dying again. Now please, I'd like to rest before I die. I need to prepare myself before I finally see my mother."

Just as he rests his head on the pillow, as if he is about to turn in for the night, the comrade sits up, looking at Yohan. "Just in case, would you make sure that I die this time? And that nobody comes to revive me?"

Yohan nods.

"Thank you," he says as he lies back down. "Goodbye, dongmu."

The comrade closes his eyes, his hands folded over his stomach. This time Yohan waits for longer. Afterward, he takes the comrade's pulse and confirms that his heart has stopped. He opens the door, goes downstairs, and exits the building. Just as he approaches the café racer, he looks around and waits. He gives it another five minutes, watching the door to the flat. Once he has ensured that no one enters the building, he turns on the motorcycle and revs the engine.

CHAPTER 8

The Exiled

WE STAY IN A HOUSE RENTED BY THE RECONNAISSANCE Bureau. It is small and cramped with a low ceiling that leaves barely any space above our heads. But it is fully furnished, ready to be moved into, and we are given a monthly stipend. Common areas are on the first floor. Two bedrooms are on the second floor. I take one and he takes one.

Every morning, Doha wakes up first. He goes for a jog and then makes coffee, which is when I get up. He hands me a cup with a dash of milk, as I prefer, and we walk out together to catch the bus to the campus. His Ph.D. is in economics, while mine is in psychology. We try not to talk to anyone. If we are to talk to professors or fellow students, we must inform our security detail from the Reconnaissance Bureau, who will assess our situation with State Security before the Great Leader approves contact.

Doha disregards all this. He goes out every night. I don't think he even gets any work done. I know he goes to classes, but I have yet to really see him study. All the books he ever has with him are novels. I don't know how he is getting away with this, but it is not my problem. I have my own things to do. My parents are expecting much of me. Having been selected directly by the Leader is a high honour. I must live up to it.

One morning, Doha comes over to me at the kitchen table, where I'm highlighting key points in a research paper and taking notes. He puts his palm down on the page I'm reading. "I'm sick and tired of seeing you, day in day out, just spending your time indoors or at the library. Come on, let's go out. You do know that all this work is not necessary?"

I look up, my mouth gaping in disbelief. "What do you mean?" I answer his Korean with English. "Also, we're supposed to study and practise our foreign languages. I'd appreciate if you cared."

Doha shakes his head and switches to English. "You really think that we're here to learn the great wisdom of the West and apply it back home?"

"That's what we were told."

"C'mon, let's get out of here."

"What about the security detail? Surely they won't just —"

"I gave them a hundred quid each and told them to enjoy themselves. We should too."

"A hundred quid? But I thought our allowance was —"

"Hongjin, you're going to kill me with all these questions. I'm trying to do something for you here."

I have to admit, I was curious. I give myself a few minutes to dress, just a simple long skirt and turtleneck. I put a long coat on top. "You look like a nun on a day out," Doha says. I punch him in the shoulder.

We walk over to St. Clement's Street just as a bus passes with a loud honk, trying to get a cab in front to get a move on. I flinch and Doha laughs. "See? You look more alive already."

I twist my lips in displeasure at him.

"You hungry?" he asks.

"Sure."

"All right, let's get some food in you, then."

We walk one street over to Cowley, where he takes me to a restaurant called Le Taj, which I find very puzzling because "Le" is French.

"It exudes elegance and class," Doha says when I ask about it while waiting for our food.

"I don't get how mixing languages gives elegance. We'd call that a bastardization back home."

The dishes arrive. Butter chicken, tikka masala, lamb korma, and a bowl of basmati rice. The food is filling and hearty. It's spicy, smooth, and delicious all at the same time, and I am astonished at how many different flavours I am able to experience from just a single dish.

"Do you come here often?"

"This is one of my favourite places around here."

A middle-aged Indian man comes out from the kitchen and seems to recognize Doha. They exchange a few words in English, and then the Indian man asks Doha, pointing at me, if I'm his girlfriend. He shakes his head and says that we're just on a first date. After the man walks off to tend to another table, I lean in to protest. "This is not a date!"

"I'm kidding. I know this isn't."

"Don't joke about it!"

"Who's going to know? Who's going to go back to Pyongyang all the way from Oxford and say you had a fake date with me at an Indian restaurant for the sole purpose of, I don't know, ruining your chances at marrying a high-ranking military officer or one of those old wrinkled party members?"

"I know but —"

"Just relax. No one's watching. No one's listening. That's the point. I came out here not for the sake of the republic but for myself. You can suffocate all you want back home, but out here, just try to breathe a bit, will you?"

Once we are done, he pulls out a fifty-quid note and slaps it on the table. I don't bother asking questions anymore. We continue down Cowley and then High Street, where students are out in groups, flocking in and out of places. Doha randomly chooses a pub and I follow him. Inside, it is very crowded. People are talking and I find it almost deafening how the chatter just piles on top of itself. He asks me what I want, and I shake my head in confusion. He goes to the bar to order while I manage to find a small corner table with two high stools. Doha floats over, holding two large glasses filled with black liquid and a bit of foam on top.

"What's that?"

"It's beer."

"This is beer? It's black."

"It's beer, I assure you."

I take a drink. It is far too creamy, and there is a deep bitterness to it accompanied by what I can only describe as the taste of coffee or maybe chocolate. Dark chocolate would make sense, considering the colour. To my surprise, I finish it quite quickly. It has an addicting taste. Doha chuckles and goes to the bar to get two more.

"You ever thought about what you want to do when you leave here?" he asks me.

"Leave? What do you mean?"

"Leave Oxford. Our programs will be done at some point, and then we'll have to go back."

"I suppose I'll obtain a position in the party," I say.

"Is there a position you want in particular? I can help you."

"I'll handle it myself, thank you."

"How about going abroad?"

"Is that even possible?"

"Yeah. You know, this isn't my first time abroad. I was actually educated in Switzerland. That's where I spent most of my teenage years."

That explains his cavalier attitude. It is an abnormal privilege for anyone from the republic to be raised abroad. He is practically royalty.

"I had this private tutor who taught me mathematics when I was in a high school in Geneva. He was a professor at the local university and he was from the republic."

"How did he get his position in Switzerland?"

"When Kim Pyong-il, the Leader's eldest son, was ousted by his brother, he was sent on diplomatic positions in Europe. They wanted someone to keep an eye on him, so they placed this professor in Switzerland to watch Kim Pyong-il. A large donation to the university did the trick. Or so I was told."

"And he also taught you mathematics."

"Yeah, I wasn't doing particularly well in mathematics, so my mother asked for a favour. I'd go to his home and we would go through math problems. And there was this man in the corner always watching, who I assumed was from the Bureau because that was literally all he did. Just watch."

He lifts his glass to his lips, his eyes distant while he muses, but then changes his mind and puts it down. "There was this one time, though, the agent assigned to us was not there. I think there was a more urgent matter going on, and that was the night he told me how he had left behind his entire family in the South during the war. They were all in Busan, but he went to his family home in Yonan to recover some valuables. Heirlooms, like his grandfather's watch, his mother's necklace, passed down through generations, as well as mementos, like the only pictures he had of his parents, forgotten in the hubbub of fleeing. By that time, the UN had pushed the North all the way to the Chinese border, and he, like almost everyone then, was certain it was over. When he got to Yonan, it was the winter of the Battle of Chosin Reservoir and the Chinese were pouring in. By the time the January–Fourth Retreat happened, he got stuck there. The Chinese had forced the UN past the thirty-eighth, and Seoul was lost once more. It all happened so fast. He hoped that the UN would at least push up to where he was, but they never did. So, he never saw his family again. He was a smart man, though. University educated. Took posts at the Kim Il Sung University and became the party's watchdog for an ill-favoured sibling of the Leader."

"Is he still there? In Switzerland?"

"No, he died a few years ago. He tried to defect. Ran from his apartment in Geneva to the South Korean embassy. He never made it. The next day, he was on the news: 'North Korean man killed in a traffic accident.' A hit and run."

He flashes a crooked smile at me, like he is tasting something bitter and is trying to pretend it is delicious. After a pause he swiftly drinks the remainder of his stout and wipes his mouth.

I break the silence. "Do you think they killed him?"

Doha laughs. "Of course they killed him. They kill everyone who tries to run. Especially if you're important."

I look around uncomfortably as he says this.

"Don't worry, for fuck's sake. Relax. We're fine."

"How do you know? You just said —"

"Look at us. We are drinking Guinness, our bellies full of Indian food, in the middle of Oxford. This is a gift, Hongjin. Enjoy it. It's not gonna last forever. And if it's all going to end by a firing squad, or a car running you over one day, why bother being careful?"

Once again I have nothing to say to that. From that night on, we go to more dinners and pubs. My papers sometimes remain unread for days. It is not that I start to care less, but there is a feeling that I get when I'm with Doha. With him I am able to relax and allow my mind to rest, to drift away. It's intoxicating.

The Rejected

The woman takes out a green soju bottle from the cooler, goes behind the counter to pick out an extra shot glass, and rejoins Yunah.

"I don't want any," Yunah says.

But the woman ignores her and pours two shots. She drinks hers, raising her glass for a lonely toast. She pours another for herself. "Come on, you're not seriously going to let me drink by myself?"

"I prefer to stay clear-headed during all this."

"Yet when you were running that pub of yours, you were drinking constantly."

"It was part of the job, and I did not drink constantly. Just enough to get the conversation going."

"Conversations with him?"

"Junichi?" Yunah asks.

"Yes, Junichi. I hate that name. Doha had his reasons for preferring Japanese names, but I like Korean names better. It's concise. Like your name, Seonhye Park."

Yunah tilts her head back.

"Or is it Yunah Choi?"

Yunah coughs, trying to dislodge what feels like mucus stuck in her throat.

"I've watched you for a while," the woman continues. "I've seen you observe him. I've seen you follow him. I've seen how he intrigues you."

"I'm not intrigued by your guy. It's my job."

"Intrigue or not, you intrigued me. When Doha mentioned you at the Magpie in a report, I sensed something was off, so I dug a little deeper. You were born in Seoul, went to Munrae Elementary School, Sinseo Middle School, and an international Christian high school. Was that where you learned English? Is that why your Korean accent is nonexistent? Or perhaps you really lost your accent when you went to the University of Toronto, majoring in biology. Then afterwards, Queen's School of Medicine. I appreciated all of that, the details to throw off the lack of Koreanness in you. Normally, one would stop there, but you see, I had a feeling about you. I only needed to contact a few sleeper agents in Seoul to find out you're not from there. No birth certificate. No national ID number. Not a trace of Seonhye Park in this world. Just a made-up name attached to a convincing enough face."

Yunah's fingers start digging into her palm as she makes fists on her knees.

"Your superiors evidently thought it was okay to throw you into this role, and they also likely assumed that people would just buy it. See your face, hear your name — it all matches up in their mind and the flaws and inconsistencies just disappear. Your fluent English, your lack of knowledge of the culture, your Western mannerisms. I do find Americans easy to work around. Your prejudices are so predictable and so sticky. They're like blueprints to how you work."

Yunah tries to sift through her memory to recall any mention of a woman during the op, but she comes up short. She is unable to recognize this woman's face or her likeness in any of the data she has gathered.

"You do know who I am, don't you?" the woman asks.

Yunah can't believe their biggest blind spot was to assume Dr. Ryu was a man just because they thought it would be impossible for a woman in the North to rise to such a status. "I know you," Yunah says. "I've seen your dossier."

"Oh, the dossier. Sure, you know what to call me. What I've done. What I can do. But you don't know anything below the surface. While I know the real you. Yunah. Yunah Choi. It's a very pretty name, by the way," Dr. Ryu says.

Yunah frowns.

"Born in Nassau County. Parents ran a bagel store. Still running a bagel store, I believe."

"How do you know this?"

"Patience and determination."

"I don't see the benefit of knowing who I am. I'm nothing."

"Oh, but the benefits are endless. Details of where one was born and raised all add up to paint a full picture. My research allowed me to arrive at Yunah Choi, the American, without ever having to meet you or talk to you."

"So what? It's not like you can use that information for anything."

"Actually, it is very important to me. Because he wrote about you, the one you call Junichi. He mentioned you in his reports. At first I thought he was just doing his due diligence to know all the Americans in the area. But then he went to you over and over again for no strategic advantage. I thought he was trying to develop a rapport with you to keep you close and use this closeness as leverage. After all, he has never had anyone other than his handlers in his life. No friends and certainly no lovers. Yet he took interest in you. I wonder why."

"Maybe he was observing me, just like how I was observing him."

"Possible," Dr. Ryu tips her head. "And you?"

"Like I said, he was the mission. Nothing more."

"He'd be disappointed to hear this."

"I don't care."

Dr. Ryu seems to ignore this comment, taking her shot and pouring another one for herself. The other glass remains full. Yunah tries to not look at it. "Where is he now?" she asks.

"I've sent him away. I have no use for him anymore and I don't want him to die in this purge. I worry about him, which brings me back to you. He needs guidance. A comrade."

"Right, a comrade," Yunah sneers. "He can fend for himself."

"Of course he can. He's my protege. And Doha's. He is utterly brilliant. I believe in him as much as I have believed in anything in my life. But I'm not the gambling type. I like assurances. So I'm asking you for one."

"How exactly am I going to do that?"

"I'm sure you have your ways. I just want you to watch over him, whether from close up or afar. Just ensure that he is safe."

"What's in it for me?"

"You will be able to bring me in."

"You're turning yourself in?"

"As long as you agree to what I'm suggesting."

"Why?" Yunah asks. "What's the play? How are you fucking me?"

"There is no play. It's just that my time has come. The purge will naturally run its course and take me as well. I'm giving you all of me for his freedom and safety. It has to be you. You've talked with him for long enough. You've studied him and you know him. You may think you only know of his false identity, but trust me, he gave you a lot of himself in those conversations. More than you think."

Yunah finally picks up the drink and washes it down in one go. Surprisingly, it tastes fresh, even sweet. "I'll think about it."

•

From the moment she touches down in Oxford, she becomes Seonhye Park.

The pub is a nice setup. It's cozy with intimate lighting that glows orange in the darkened atmosphere. The city is what she had imagined. Richly decorated structures with centuries of history now used for mundane purposes, winding streets that are just wide enough for two cars to pass.

They first stake out the flat the North Korean operatives are staying in. She and Thomas wait in various rotating positions outside the building and count who goes in and out of the small two-storey building. When they have all the pictures, they return to their quarters at the pub and line up the photos with various faces in the database.

Only one of them is officially identified. Doha Kim. Rumoured to be part of the family, he's the big draw. The rest of them are a faceless blur. Low-ranking foot soldiers and sleepers that appear and disappear. But they are all photographed, documented, and cross-checked in the databases. Some are Chinese on paper; some are Japanese or Vietnamese. None are ever South Korean. Doha Kim and one subordinate seem to live in the flat. The others come and go.

Before the Magpie opened, the Americans studied their targets' routines. Around six in the morning, the two North Koreans come out for a jog. At around nine they leave the flat and walk to the Department of Economics building. Doha is well known to them due to his public connection to the university. He is an alumnus, which means he has access to the facilities, and his status as a novelty guest lecturer grants him a certain reverence despite him not holding an official position among faculty. He goes to lunches with other professors; he attends banquets and parties. Meanwhile, under the guise of a graduate student at the university, Junichi keeps mostly to himself, maintaining minimal contact with outsiders. When not in class, he goes to the library and to cafés, only to be on his laptop most of the time. Both men keep irregular schedules during the day. Sometimes the subordinate disappears for a while. But the one constant is the Soju Club. When Yunah and Thomas are ordered to investigate the restaurant, they find nothing of any use. The owner is simply an immigrant from South Korea, a young man in his mid-twenties.

"He's a bit young. Isn't that strange? Young guy owning a restaurant. It takes a lot of money to run a place. He's South Korean, but it's probably a cover," Thomas says one day as they flip through files just before they open the pub.

"They never choose South Korean as a cover."

"Why not? It's the natural choice, no? North Korean, South Korean."

"They just never have. It's not in the records."

"Well, maybe they have this time."

Thomas continues to be suspicious of the Soju Club. Yunah pushes back because she feels he only presses the issue based on the fact that they're all Korean. But she is also curious. The first time she enters the Soju Club is at lunch hour, much earlier than when the North Koreans are usually there. The owner greets her with a smile, guides her to one of the tables, and hands her a menu. His accent reminds her of her father, perhaps when he was younger. He hurriedly goes into the kitchen, leaving her with a short but kind "I'll be back."

When the owner is out of sight, she looks around and examines the interior. There is nothing special about it except that it is well put together. There are rectangular tables and white plastic chairs, and the menu is written on a black chalkboard hanging against a brick wall. There's a counter with a cash register, and a kitchen beyond it. It is a textbook cover, so obvious that it makes her doubt whether the owner is connected to any of it at all. But it is a Korean restaurant, the only one in the city, that just happens to attract the patronage of two North Korean spies. Perhaps all this is just a simple series of coincidences lining up too perfectly.

As Yunah is in the middle of these thoughts, the bell chimes and someone enters the restaurant. She looks over and immediately withdraws her gaze. It's Junichi Nakamura, the subordinate. He walks right up to the counter, craning his neck toward the small window into the kitchen to check for the owner. This is the closest she has been to their target, and she has to suppress her desire to look up again, which she eventually does and immediately finds him staring back. She gives a smile to which he responds in kind.

"The sundubu is good," he says.

"Excuse me?"

"I said the sundubu is good."

"You've had it before?"

"Wouldn't be recommending it if I hadn't."

"Thanks, I'll give it a try," she says. This is the first contact, and Yunah wants to keep it going. "He said he'll return soon."

"Did he?" he responds. "How long ago?"

"Maybe a minute or so. I could pass him a message if you're in a hurry."

"No, I'm not in a hurry." He flashes a smile and turns back.

Yunah tries to find any way to continue the conversation. "Are you from here?"

Junichi turns around again with a puzzled look on his face, but he maintains his courtesy. "No, I'm not."

"Student?"

"Yeah."

"At the university?"

"Yeah."

The short answers frustrate her, but it is expected that he would say as little as possible. She feels that if she does not make a connection with him now, it will only become more difficult. "I work at a pub in town," she blurts out, unprompted.

"Which one?"

"The Magpie."

"I've seen that place. Is it new?"

"Well, it's just changed owners," Yunah says.

"Are you studying here as well?"

"Not really, I'm just here working and travelling."

"So you're not from here?"

"No, I'm from Korea." Yunah recites her profile. "From Seoul." In that moment she sees a slight shift in his face, unnoticeable to someone not paying attention. "And you? Where are you from?"

"I'm from —" He seems to hesitate momentarily. "I'm from France."

"France?" she says, trying to act surprised despite knowing all this. "I didn't expect that."

"Right," he says. "I'm also Japanese. Is that closer to what you expected?"

"Much closer."

He laughs.

"Seonhye," she says finally, noticing that he has lowered his guard. "My name is Seonhye Park."

"Seonhye," he repeats. There is no awkwardness in his pronunciation of the name. "I'm Junichi. Junichi Nakamura."

The owner comes out then and sees Junichi. They greet each other warmly, and Junichi explains how his professor forgot to pay the bill from the night before. He settles the bill, tells the owner that he'll see him tonight, and then goes toward the door to leave.

"Hey," she says, just as he is about to pass her. "Come by the pub. First drink is on me."

"I will," he says with a smile and a nod.

When the owner comes by her table to take her order, she asks for the sundubu. The dish comes in fifteen minutes, hot and boiling in a black stone bowl. She takes a mouthful once the soup has cooled off a bit. It is indeed delicious.

The Nameless

The café racer storms through the streets. Traffic has thinned out at night, allowing him to go faster than normal. The engine's buzzing roar fills his ears as he leans into the tight corners of the winding roads. He circles around slow-moving cabs and jolts pedestrians from their evening strolls as they are just about to cross the road.

The wind is heavy against his face, but Yohan speeds up because it is the only way to calm his mind from spiralling into a web of questions. He wants to obey Dr. Ryu's last order to the letter. If she wants him to simply go, he will. As the comrade told him, Yohan can go anywhere. He has been taught to be a perpetual chameleon, to disappear from one place and pop up in another as if he always belonged there.

Once he is beyond the city limits and is about to get onto the M40, he pulls off to the side. On a patch of grass just beyond the edge of the road, he sits with his legs crossed. A double-decker coach bus bound for London zooms by. He can follow the bus south to London and make a life there. He can hide as a wage worker in a shop owned by an Asian immigrant who would pay in cash and ask no questions. Or he can take the M40 the opposite way, go to Birmingham, Leeds, or all the way up to Glasgow. Across the channel there are hundreds of cities, all teeming with networks of immigrants, legal and illegal, who look like him and can provide a great cover. As long as he keeps his head down, he can go anywhere. The possibilities are endless.

The problem is that none of those places inspire much feeling in him. It's as if they have given him yet another place to go for a mission. He used to feel differently. During the nights he spent with Doha drinking at the Soju Club, Doha would tell him stories of his numerous travels. Where he went, what he saw, whom he talked to, and Yohan absorbed all of it hungrily. At some point, he desired to see these places himself. Now he doesn't want to leave Oxford, the place he would return to after every mission. It is where Doha would give him a pat on the back, then take him to the Soju Club. Over food and a bottle of soju, everything would become familiar and calm. His mind would be able to rest from the constant vigilance. Doha's presence would fill his heart with comfort.

"Confused?" He hears Doha, seeing him sitting next to him on the grass.

"I'm not sure. It's a mix of things."

"It's the lack of sleep. Didn't I tell you? Sleep deprivation is our biggest enemy."

Doha smiles at him and points at Yohan's heart. "You're finally feeling it, the weight of being your own self."

"My own self?"

"Until now it was Dr. Ryu and me who carried the burden of your existence. We gave your life purpose, and now that we are not here to do that for you, you are overwhelmed with choice. It is what we all must go through. You have to learn one day."

"There's no time. It's too late for me to learn these things."

"Too late, coming from a such a youngster. Yohan, the world is not a place to fear and cower from. It is a place to discover who you are. Time is of no importance. No one ever has enough time. You simply stumble forward, with each stride carrying its own special mistake."

"I can't do this without you."

"But you have to. You have to find your own way."

"I don't know what to do. I know nothing outside of this life. What am I supposed to look for? What do I fight for?"

Doha puts his hand on Yohan's back. "Forget country, forget loyalty, forget whatever we put on your shoulders. Go out there and figure it out. Throw yourself into the waves of life. Be surprised, be joyful, be scared, be sad, be all of it. This is why we've brought you here. To set you free. You make the orders now, not me, not Hongjin. It's your call."

Another coach bus passes by with a guttural roar, and Yohan snaps his head up, awake. A trail of drool has come down his mouth in his brief slumber. He wipes it away with his sleeve and stands up.

All his life, he was told that everything would be fine if he just obeyed. When questions arose, he simply bottled them up, but they were still there, brooding in the corner, silently pleading with him to recognize them. Eventually, he knew he would have to deal with them.

What do I live for?

The answer is surprisingly simple. He gets on the bike, does a U-turn, and heads back to Oxford.

CHAPTER 9

The Exiled

IT IS THE THIRD YEAR OF MY SERVICE AS THE STATE Security's social behaviour advisor, a position that was created for me when I came back from Oxford with a Ph.D. in psychology. For many months, I have been shadowing officers interrogating prisoners, and I am quite excited to be given my first case of handling a possible reactionary. Until now the work has been dull, mainly signing off on mundane things such as increasing training for the military or political education classes for students.

I'm taken by a convoy of cars to Manpo, followed by trucks full of soldiers. It is a city with a large steel mill. I read the brief and learn that the manager of the mill, along with a few of the senior employees, tried to smuggle some steel to the Chinese. One had snitched, and they were all subsequently arrested. My task is to investigate and make a recommendation for the final verdict.

I have a brief chat with the commander in charge at the local Social Security Forces branch before the thieving manager is dragged out of his cell and into the interrogation room. He is beaten and mangled. I take a closer look at all the places he has been hit, slashed, and torn into. There are burn marks on his forearms. He is wearing bandages soaked in red around some of his fingertips where they pulled his nails off. His face looks like an assembly of bruised apples.

"Did you have to torture him so much? I can't really talk to him like this."

"Shall I pump him full of painkillers, madam?"

"No, never mind. Just leave us."

The commander leaves, and I am left with the prisoner in the room, his hands bound by chains. He is dressed in grey pants with a white shirt, ripped in places and smudged with blood everywhere. I stand in front of him, arms crossed. He is spent and barely even acknowledges me. I frown. I had told them that I would prefer to conduct interrogations before the torture. Pain never gives clarity. They'll confess to things that have nothing to do with them because they want it to stop.

"This is a simple matter," I begin. "You stole from the republic and therefore the Leader. So my question is, why? What was the cause?"

After a long silence, I try to look into his eyes to see if he has heard me, but his face is hidden by his hair, damp and curled. Or maybe he is dead. It happens sometimes. Their heart stops because their body has been broken down over the course of the torture. Just as I'm about to call for the guard outside, he speaks, keeping his head down. "We needed food."

"Food?"

"There was a Chinese smuggler who promised us corn in exchange for steel. So we took his offer."

"Are you insane? Pilfering the Dear Leader's resources? The very resources he needs to carry out his great revolutionary war against capitalists? Have you lost your mind?"

"No, we did it for the Leader."

"For the Leader? How bold of you to say that. Explain your logic."

"The workers were collapsing on-site because they were starving. Our production levels were going down. I needed to find a way to get some more food, so that we could work and make our Leader happy."

"Why are you lying to me? Starving? No one in this republic starves."

"Our grain rations were cut by half."

"Lies! Everyone, including this city, received six hundred grams of grain per person per day this past month, just as the month before. That is the way it works for everyone. That is the system we have."

"That is not what we got."

"Are you questioning the republic's records? Are you questioning the integrity of the Leader?"

"No, I am not. I'm simply saying we didn't have enough to eat. We were becoming weaker by the day."

"Then why did you not ask someone from the party to look into it? Why wait until now?"

"We did, but nothing happened. We were told to make do and to keep our quotas up."

"So you opted to steal. Are you making an excuse for your transgression?"

"We had no choice. We were going to miss our quota anyway," he pleads through heavy breathing.

"Or perhaps there is a more sinister plot here that you're trying to hide." I lean down and study his face. He finally lifts his head and I stare directly into his eyes. "Maybe you stole the grain. And in the process of trying to make up for the differences, you made a very stupid decision."

"No."

"Capitalist desires make one practise deceit."

"I have no such desires. I only have the desire to please our Leader. I will do anything for him. Please! I did all of this for the love of our Dear Leader! Search my home! There is nothing there!" he cries out.

One way or the other, he will be executed, because I know he is lying. The current distribution is six hundred grams of grain per day per person. In any case, there is nothing more to hear from this man. I call for the guards, and they pull him out of the chair. Two guards each hold him by an arm, letting his feet drag on the concrete floor. As he leaves, he proclaims his innocence, desperately howling, his hoarse voice scratching the air. I make my recommendations to the party official who has been put in charge of deciding his fate. I write that his motives were personal, selfish, and capitalistic and label him as a reactionary.

Bureaucracy moves swiftly to deliver justice. The following day, along with several other co-conspirators, he is driven to the city square in a truck. They are tied to posts for everyone to see. An officer loudly announces their crime of stealing from the Great Leader. The crowd murmurs. Machine gunners line up, and on the mark of the officer, they blast their weapons into the prisoners, who instantly go limp on the posts, their torsos slumped over.

The morning after, there is a protest by hundreds of labourers at the steel mill. They cry that the manager did nothing wrong and was executed for no reason. In the afternoon the military arrives. It breaks up the protest by rolling tanks right over the workers, crushing their bodies. Soldiers shoot into the crowd until none are left standing. When they are done, families flock to their dead and scream into the sky in grief. I can hear them crying from the temporary office they have set up for me. I can see them, covered in the blood and flesh of their loved ones.

I later discover, through my own investigations, that they indeed received only three hundred grams of grain per person per day for many months. There was a crop failure and grain production was down. All this information had been tucked away and suppressed by the party. I think about including this in my report, but I decide to bury it. I know very well that there is nothing to be done.

From this point on, I develop an obsession in tracking down the source of every piece of information that lands on my desk, so often and so diligently that eventually a superior officer within State Security tells me calmly that I should stay within my boundaries. It is a warning that I am far too nosy. I give him the most reassuring promise to keep unnecessary suspicions away. Lying is better than revealing the doubts that have started to form in my mind.

The Rejected

Around midnight Yunah starts to feel like she must do something. It has been too long since the blond and the bearded one went out to search for the South Korean. She tried calling, but no one has picked up. She sent a text message to let them know that Dr. Ryu is at the Soju Club, but that was about twenty minutes ago.

"Your friends are late," Dr. Ryu says.

"They'll be here soon."

"Something's gone wrong, don't you think?"

Yunah is trying to hide the uneasiness creeping over her. She decides to call it in to Cole. Before she can finish dialing her phone, she sees a black Volkswagen skid onto the curb in front of the restaurant. The car is crumpled in the front and there are bullet holes on the front hood and windshield, the glass having spider-webbed from points of impact. Deoksu exits and kicks the door in. Yunah sees him with a pistol in hand and she instinctively grabs her Glock 42, her finger on the trigger, and steps in front of Dr. Ryu. She notices that Deoksu is holding the bearded one's gun.

"Where is he?" he shouts, his weapon raised and aimed straight at her.

"He's not here."

"I'm talking about Jihoon. Where is he? Why isn't he here?"

"He's —" Yunah hesitates. "He's gone."

He blinks rapidly as he processes this. "He's what?"

"He's dead."

"Ssibal, what? Gaessibal, how is he dead?" His voice goes up with each word. "How the fuck is Jihoon-i hyung dead?"

"Stray bullet. When my colleague was trying to shoot you."

"Where's the body?"

"In the kitchen."

"Show me."

"I'm not moving," Yunah says.

"Jihoon-i hyung, are you there?" he shouts.

"I told you, he's dead."

His eyes quickly dart toward the kitchen. He steps sideways, and Yunah turns her body with him, keeping herself in between him and Dr. Ryu. He moves until he can peer over the counter and see Jihoon's body. His breathing gets rough.

"You Americans," he says, almost in a mutter. "I've been here five years, and you mess everything up in one day. You fucking Americans."

For a while they stand, pointing their weapons at each other.

"You borrowed that?" she asks, gesturing toward the gun with her head.

"Yeah," he says curtly.

"What did you do to them?"

"You killed Jihoon. I don't care what happens to those Yankee fucks."

"It was an accident. We didn't mean to."

"I should kill you. I really should, but I won't. I just want Dr. Ryu," Deoksu says.

"You'll leave here alive. That's my counter-offer," Yunah says.

"I have no problem shooting both of you right now. I'm going to ask again. Hand over Dr. Ryu."

"You think I won't shoot back?"

She has his head right at the edge of her iron sight. She knows she has a shot. It is close enough that she won't miss.

"It's all right," Dr. Ryu says quietly. "Let me go."

Yunah steps back, pressing herself slightly against Dr. Ryu. "Stay behind me."

"Let me go," Dr. Ryu repeats. "It's easier this way. No one else has to get hurt tonight." She rests her hand on top of Yunah's pistol and gently presses it downward. She inches toward the edge of the barrel of Deoksu's gun, shielding Yunah. She looks back. "Remember what we talked about."

Deoksu slants his pistol to maintain a clear shot on Yunah and starts backing away, with Dr. Ryu following him slowly. Only when Deoksu has his back to the door does he lower his weapon. He lets Dr. Ryu out first. They get in the beaten-up Volkswagen and drive away.

•

The first time Junichi visits the Magpie, Yunah is surprised to see that Doha is with him. Junichi comes up to the bar. She exchanges basic pleasantries with him and talks a little about whisky. He orders his drinks and takes them back to the table. Junichi does not come back to the bar to talk to her during that night, but the fact that they managed to get Doha Kim in the bar excites the team.

The second time Junichi visits, it is the weekend and he is alone.

"Where's your friend?" she asks him.

"He's not a friend."

"Who is he, then?"

"A mentor."

"He decided to skip drinks for tonight?"

He thinks for a moment. "He said he's tired. He's turned in."

But he hasn't. Thomas confirmed not too long ago that he is at a park, taking a leisurely stroll.

"What would you like?"

"I'm not sure."

"You don't have a preference for something?"

"I'll drink anything."

"Ah, you're one of those."

She makes him an old-fashioned. Very strong. Double the whisky. She has learned a few cocktail recipes for the mission, and this is her favourite drink to make. She tops the whole thing off with an orange peel on a toothpick and passes him the drink. He takes a sip and winces slightly at its strength, but he smacks his lips, content with the taste. He raises the glass in her direction to show his satisfaction.

"You like it?"

"I love it."

"I'll keep that in mind, then, for next time."

They talk about how she is from Korea. He has many questions, and Yunah tries to answer them as much as she can. For the sake of making the character come alive, she takes the liberty of using parts from her own life, such as her parents and conversations with Korean classmates from university, to create Seonhye. He absorbs everything with the eagerness of a small child. Sometimes she adds tidbits about her grandmother for some authenticity because everything she says about her grandmother is true. "My grandma used to call me ddong-gangaji."

"What does that mean?"

"Means shit puppy."

He laughs at that.

She asks him about his upbringing. His childhood growing up in Nantes. He talks about the landmarks there, like the large mechanical elephant. He enjoyed the relative peace of it compared to a big city. With subtle glances, she keeps track of his drink. Once he reaches the bottom of his glass, she suggests another one. He says he wants to try a beer.

Yunah holds up her finger as she goes to the cooler to retrieve a bottle she has in mind. "You're going to love this one."

She pours it into a small beer glass, the foam fizzing on top. She can smell the sweet aroma wafting from the beer. The first time she tried it, it obliterated her sense of what beer should be. It is spicy, with a tone of vanilla — sweet, fruity, and more.

Junichi takes a sip. "Gouden Carolus Tripel," he reads from the label. "Thank you. This is very good."

"An import from Belgium."

He smiles at her. Now that she has him comfortable, Yunah thinks of ways to get him to talk about himself.

"You know, we shouldn't be friends, according to history," she says.

"What do you mean?"

"Well, our ancestors fought a lot. And your country colonized us at some point."

"But I don't really feel Japanese. I'm more French than Japanese."

"Yet you are." She draws a circle in the air around his face with her finger. "All of this very much comes from there." She playfully leans on the bar and looks at him in a teasing way, trying to see if he might break his reticence.

"So you're saying that I can only be your friend if I reject who I am?"

Yunah doesn't know what to say. This is not an answer she expected. She needs to get him to open up but not like this. "I'm messing with you. I don't care who you are. Japanese, Korean, Chinese, Singaporean, it doesn't matter. What does it matter in the end? Anyways, we all look the same in the eyes of others."

But Junichi smiles at her and takes a last sip of the beer. Instead of asking him what he wants, Yunah brings out two shot glasses and a bottle of Irish whiskey. She pours out two shots. "With this, we're friends, no matter what we are."

They cheers and drink.

The evening stretches on for a while, and they continue to talk about nothing in particular. Toward the end of the night, Junichi moves to pay. As he counts out his cash onto the bar, he pauses and looks at her. "Why did your grandmother call you shit puppy? Did she not like you?"

"No, she loved me. She came to live with us to help my parents, but also because she wanted to be closer to me. She told me that when you fawn over your kids too much, when you call them all sorts of cute and nice things, the ghosts get jealous and they put curses on them. She said that a long time ago, people called their children not very nice things. Like 'mot-nan' as in ugly, or 'mib-sang' as in troublemaker, or 'gae-ddong' as in dog poop, or 'ddong-gangaji.'"

"As in shit puppy," he says.

They both laugh.

"You must have loved your grandmother very much."

"Yes, I did."

The truth is that she doesn't know whether she loved her grandmother. Her grandmother's love was something she took, and she had no thoughts about whether she had to give back any of it. Even as her grandmother spent most of her days in front of the TV and taking walks by herself, Yunah was far too occupied with school and her extracurricular activities.

Not long after returning to Korea, Yunah's grandmother passed away in her sleep in her Samcheonpo apartment. Yunah couldn't go to the funeral with her parents. She had her SAT. It was years later, when she was feeling crippling isolation in university, that it struck her that her grandmother was lonely during those days. Instead of being holed up in her own room, she could have joined her to watch Korean dramas or take evening strolls through the neighbourhood park. She could have traded a small bit of the time she had reserved for her future to be with her grandmother. But she realized all this too late. And there was no one else to call her shit puppy to keep the ghosts away.

The Nameless

Just as he passes through a wooded area on Headington Road, he runs into a car wreck, the vehicle's headlights still beaming into the darkness. He stops and approaches. To the right the blue iron gates to Headington Hill Park are wide open, though they should be closed at this time. He sees that the car was hit on the right side, having spun in a half circle after impact. Someone had opened the gate, hid their car from sight, and waited for just the right time to ram the other car from the side as it came down Headington. At least that is what he can gather.

Yohan sees the two Americans inside. Yunah is not among them. He recognizes the driver to be the one subdued by Deoksu earlier. He checks his pulse and sees that he is still breathing. When he goes around to the passenger side, to the blond, her head is laid back on the headrest, a trail of blood streaming down just past the front of her ear. A thick whiff of gasoline is in the air, and he sees smoke building beneath the crumpled hood of the car. Yohan pulls her out from the wreckage, dragging her past the curb and leaning her against a fence. He goes back to the vehicle and pulls out the bearded man after prying off the crushed door. As soon as he moves the two of them to safety from the vehicle, he calls emergency services, notifying them of a car accident.

He checks to see if they have any weapons. The bearded one's chest holster is empty. He goes to the blond, pats around her hips, and finds that her sidearm has also been taken. Their phones are missing as well.

"You." He hears a quiet mutter as he checks for any wounds that need to be taken care of immediately. He pats her just under the chest, and she sharply groans. Her ribs are broken.

"Don't move," Yohan says. "An ambulance is on its way."

He feels a tug at his jacket and sees that she is trying to grab him. "Stop," she says, gasping in pain. "Stay," she says. "The offer still stands."

"What offer?"

"A new life." She continues to drawl in a dazed manner. "Anything you wish. Just stay."

"Who attacked you?" he asks.

"Soju Club. Guy from Soju Club."

"Jihoon?" he utters before realizing that she is talking about Deoksu.

When he hears the sirens of the ambulance nearing, Yohan gets back on the motorcycle. As he is about to start the engine, he considers for a moment. A life in America. He has thought about it before. Doha used to talk about it quite often, imagining what it would be like for him.

"I see you with a respectable degree to your name," Doha once told him over a drink at the Soju Club. "I see you with a good job that pays you enough to enjoy life. I see you with a few friends. Close friends. I don't think you're a social butterfly. I see you finding a nice girl to be by your side. Maybe like you, maybe not like you at all."

The place of the American dream, where he would be able to achieve whatever he desired, as long as he put his mind to it.

A fresh start free of all attachments of his former life. That is, this life.

"Where are you in all of that?" he had asked Doha.

"What does that matter? I'm talking about you."

"I'd like you to be in it. I want you there with me."

Doha had scoffed and shook his head. "How long do you think I'll be around, Yohan?"

If he had known that their time would run out so soon, perhaps he would have been more honest and not hidden what he felt. He was afraid that Doha would chastise him, that he had to be strong and be ready for a cruel and brutal world. Keep still, hold it in. Soft exterior, hard interior. This was the ideal that Doha espoused. This was what he wanted from Yohan.

But if Doha were still here, Yohan knows what he would say to him. That he misses him, and he wishes he was here by his side, not for his guidance but simply for his presence. That he misses his calm but witty demeanour and the way he claps as he laughs.

Yohan makes up his mind. The motorcycle roars. He rides around the wreckage and cruises down Headington Road, running the next red, with unsuspecting cars at the intersection honking in shock.

CHAPTER 10

The Exiled

THE SOUND OF JET ENGINES BLASTS ACROSS THE SKY AS I drive up to the curb in my Sungri sedan. Doha is waving at me from the exit of the terminal. It is his fifth trip this year as a foreign intelligence serviceman. His job is to attach himself to various diplomatic offices, with a dual mandate. One is to keep an eye on foreign diplomats sent out by the republic, and the other is to gather any useful intelligence on NATO countries.

In the car on the way back, he tells me about Berlin. Once torn in two, marked as East and West. Now reunified in jubilation. He tells me about the cars, how magnificent they are. Then a full-throated praise for the beers and how they gave him such a clear head in the morning.

"Beers with no hangover, imagine that! Just a beautiful country," he says.

I roll my eyes when he tells me about the women. He describes his occasional trysts with blond, blue-eyed women with buttocks unlike anything he has seen in Pyongyang.

"Gosh, you pig," I say. "Are you talking about me?"

"I wouldn't know, would I?" he says with a wink.

I shove him lightly. This is what we do now. He has all these stories from abroad, while I'm here working for State Security. After the successful operation at the steel mill, they have sent me to various places for handling "problems." They all start in similar ways. A record doesn't match, so an investigation is conducted. It's always the same issue rearing its head over and over again — people are hungry and don't have enough to eat.

It is a difficult time right now. The regime is changing and things are volatile. The Soviet Union has collapsed, which means aid is not as available as it once was. Propaganda campaigns reminding the people that this is all part of the glorious struggle against the capitalist thugs have intensified. There is no famine, and no one is dying of starvation. If anyone says so, they are arrested and imprisoned. It is instead called a march toward victory. The Arduous March.

But to Doha, it's as if all these problems belong to another country. I am also not personally affected. I am doing much better than the average citizen, wrapped in the cocoon of privilege while they suffer the brunt of it. The worst thing for me is that it is more difficult now to get wine from abroad.

We go to his place, where he brings out a bottle of whisky. He is proud of it. It is a Dalmore 35 he scored while in the U.K. He went to the distillery and inquired directly.

"Let's have a drink to celebrate my return."

We raise our glasses together and we drink. It's always a merry occasion when I drink with him. It is like the days we spent in Oxford.

"I have a favour to ask of you," I say.

"A favour? Sure."

"We'll have to go somewhere for a bit."

We finish our drinks and hop back into my car. It takes about an hour to get there. The paved road eventually turns into a dirt path. The car rocks. Doha grabs onto the handle above him. "If you were someone else, I'd think you were taking me out to an execution," he jokes, though I catch a hint of tension.

"We're almost there."

A few kilometres up the unpaved road, in the middle of a desolate field of grass and dirt, there is a small village, a collection of low buildings huddled together like a pack of animals sharing warmth. There is an orphanage, a grey concrete building five windows wide with one floor and a barren yard in front. Two of the windows are broken and have been patched with strips of clear vinyl.

I park the car right by the entrance and we get out. There is a group of children who run toward us and ask us for food. Doha has chocolate from Berlin in his pockets and distributes it to the children. Each of them runs off as soon as they get a square, presumably to savour it in peace.

"I wonder if they know this is probably the priciest thing that they'll ever hold in their entire lives," Doha says. "Where is the headmaster, anyway? He should be greeting us. If it were anyone else, we would've had him shot by now."

Probably drunk. I'm the one who provides the extra funds so he can buy all the alcohol he wants. It's part of the deal. "Wait here," I tell Doha.

As I enter the building, I am greeted with a portrait of Kim Jong-il. With no provisions coming in, somehow this new portrait has replaced the old portrait of the late Great Leader, Kim Il-sung. I turn into the hallway and open the second door. There, children are sleeping on a cold grey floor with only a thin blanket over their bodies. I spot him, wearing a rag of a shirt with torn pants, holding a piece of tree bark in his hand. His hair has grown uncontrollably, covering most of his face, which has black and brown smudges. I gently touch his shoulder to wake him up. His eyes slowly open and he sees me. I hoist him up into my arms and walk back to where Doha is in the yard. I let him down gently on the ground. He can barely stand. The boy stops chewing on his tree bark as if it is a pacifier and stares up at him.

"And who's this?" Doha says, crouching down to see the boy at eye level.

I pause because I know that from this moment on, everything will change.

"He's a Kim."

Doha jerks his body back from the boy. Blood rushes out of Doha's face as he stands frozen, staring at the boy, who goes back to chewing the piece of tree bark. "How?"

"A bastard of the late Leader."

I see his face turn from confusion to revelation.

"Your half-brother," I add.

He cups his mouth in shock, turns around, and walks away, his shoulders heaving deeply. In all my time of having known Doha, I have never seen him so distressed. I wonder if this was all a mistake.

"He was meant to die. Eliminated like the rest of them."

Doha snaps his attention back to her. "Hongjin, this is dangerous."

"Aren't you used to transgressions?" I ask.

"Yes, but they were trivial transgressions. All of them were ultimately harmless to the regime. But this — this is going to get even me in trouble."

"So help me."

"Help you? We should kill him right now."

I stand there, my fingernails anxiously digging into my palms.

"Why him? Why must he live and not the others?" Doha asks.

"Because I choose to. I choose to keep him alive."

"What is wrong with you, Hongjin? You know what we need to do. What we need to do to survive."

"Well, maybe I don't want to do it anymore. I don't want to serve these jong-ganna-ssaekkis anymore."

The last sentence comes out more forceful than I thought it would. But I know it has been there for a long time, a lump that has burst, releasing everything I've ever held down.

"When I was twelve, I used to have a best friend. We walked to school together, we ate lunch together, we were inseparable. After school I'd go to her house and sometimes she would come to mine, and we'd do homework, draw, and play. One day she disappeared. I asked my mother why. She said they went away to the countryside, and I was so heartbroken because she didn't say goodbye to me. I cried for weeks. Years later I found out that she and her parents were executed. The Leader ordered it. No one ever said what the reason was. There was no record of any crime they committed. All I found out was that they were shot in a field.

"After that I focused on duty. Whatever happened there had to be a reason because the Leader ordered it. Isn't that what we learned? The Leader is unquestionable. He is all-knowing, all-seeing. If he does something, he does it for a good reason."

Doha puts his head down in sombre acknowledgement.

"But you know what we do. I'm fed lies, and then I feed lies to others in return. So what does anything we do matter? Why does a child need to be killed? What's the reason? Because I don't believe in that kind of duty anymore. And this boy, I will save him. He will be my truth."

"I can't walk this path with you, Hongjin," Doha says while looking at the ground.

"Why not?"

"I'm not that brave. I'm already scared to death about what will come of this."

I approach him, waiting for him to raise his head and see my resolve. I take his hands in mine. They are limp, but he doesn't pull away.

"Doha, it was you who first showed me that there is more to life than duty. This boy deserves a chance. Born of circumstances and doomed for it. He is no different than us. We just ended up on the right side of it. For once in our lives, let's do something of our own. Help me give this boy a purposeful life. Help me to do this, please."

Doha finally lifts his head. His eyes are wet and red. We look at each other for a few moments before he walks to the child, who is playing in the dirt. Doha crouches down and watches him. "What are you doing?" he asks the boy.

"Building a house for the toad."

"The toad?"

"An older boy told me that if you build a house for the toad, the toad will give us a new house."

"And why do you want a new house?"

"For my friends."

"Your friends? That's generous of you."

Already I see that Doha has made up his mind. I can tell by the way he looks at the boy, from the way he pats his hair lightly.

"Let me help you, then," Doha says and starts digging a hole of his own next to the boy, his clean fingernails collecting dirt.

The Rejected

Immediately after the South Korean leaves, Yunah contemplates the situation. The blond and the bearded man are likely incapacitated or, at worst, killed. The South Korean has taken Dr. Ryu. She feels like she has been gutted and left out to dry, nothing else to do.

The soju bottle on the table still has some liquor left. She takes it and two shot glasses and goes into the kitchen, where she sits by Jihoon's body. He almost looks like he is sleeping. She pours one out for herself and one for him. "To you. I'm sorry, Jihoon."

She brings out her phone and calls her father's mobile. Around this time, he would still be at the store. It does not ring for long until he answers.

"Appa," she says.

"Yunah-ya. What's the occasion?"

"Is Eomma there?"

"Yes. Hold on, let me put her on."

She can hear him calling "Yeobo!" to her mother in the background. She can imagine the scene: her father entering the kitchen at the back, where freshly baked bagels come out of the oven, laid on a cartoonishly large spatula that she later learned from a baker was called a peel. She hears him walking past workers busily moving about in the packed kitchen, greeting them with his curt but friendly utterances of "hi," "good," and "nice work." Way in the back is a small alcove, where her mother spends half her working days diligently poring over the books — order forms, invoices, statements, employee time sheets — and whatever else she deems necessary for the business to prosper. She was a math whiz when she was a child and top of her class at law school. Those skills are now used to keep a bagel store running.

After looking into her mother's usual hiding spot, her father grumbles, wondering where she is. He asks a passing employee in the kitchen, who says, "Bathroom." Yunah recognizes the voice right away as Manuel. She recalls his puffed-up cheeks and full belly hanging slightly over his belt, a sweat-soaked bandana around his forehead. During the summers when she worked there, every morning she would ask if she could have a fresh bagel. He'd grin, tell her to wait for a moment, and then sneak one from the latest batch.

Finally, her father's call for "yeobo" yields a distant but clear "What?"

"Yunah is calling; she is asking for you."

In a few seconds, her mother is on the phone. "Yunah-ya? Something wrong?"

"I'm just calling. Why do you assume something is wrong?"

"Because you never call first. You never ever do."

"Well, nothing's wrong. I'm just calling."

There's a pause on the other end. "No, something is wrong, I can tell. I raised you all those years and I know when you're okay or not."

Yunah takes a moment to consider how to put it into words. "I'm just having a difficult time at work, but it'll all be over soon."

"Really? Work is hard?"

"It's not the best. I'm thinking of taking a break for a bit."

"Yunah-ya, hold on, are you quitting?"

She can hear her father in the background. "Quitting? Did she say she is quitting her job?"

"I didn't say I was quitting. I'm just thinking about it," Yunah says.

"Yunah-ya, think carefully," her mother says. "I never wanted to run a bagel store, but it gave us so much. It paid for your school, the house, and now our trip."

"Trip? What trip?"

"Ah, we didn't tell you! We are going on a cruise to the Mediterranean. We're going to Italy, Greece, and Turkey. I'm so excited!"

"That's great, uh, but why the Mediterranean?"

"You might not know this, but before I met your father, I was very into history. I took some courses while in university, and I always wanted to see those ancient ruins up close."

"Why didn't you ever tell me about any of this? I didn't know you were into history."

"It's what happens with everyone. There were things to do. We had to find a way to make a living here. We had to raise you. It's natural that some things you love get tossed to the side."

Much was tossed to the side from their lives. Yunah and her parents shared very little aside from the house that they lived in together. After her grandmother left, she ate alone often, her parents eating once they got back late from the shop.

But she does remember good moments. Like their outings to a sushi buffet in Flushing. It was easy to be there. No menu to agonize over. They just had to constantly pile food onto their plates to get their money's worth. Even her mother, who normally gave Yunah little jabs about how she should watch her weight, told her to eat to her heart's content. There were moments like that in their lives, however few, where all she had to do was be their daughter.

"Do you have any regrets?" she blurts out.

A short pause follows before her mother asks, "About what?"

She pauses for a second to decide whether to bring this up. "Me."

"Well, I regret not making you listen to us more."

"I listen to you all the time."

"Yes, but you never actually do."

Yunah starts to laugh and that prompts a laugh from her mother as well.

"I don't regret anything. Especially if it was for you."

"Are you just saying that?"

"I have wishes for you. I wish you would practise Korean and be fluent. I wish you would find someone nice to be with. I wish you would come back to church. I wish you would visit us more. But I don't regret anything about you. So don't ever think about that again."

Yunah wonders when the last time was that her mother's words didn't feel like needles in her ears.

"I'll come for Seollal. I promise."

"Really? Yeobo! She's coming for Seollal."

"Yunah is coming for Seollal? Wonderful!" She hears her father.

"But I'm not going to church, okay?"

"That's fine."

"Seriously, no church."

"No church. My promise for your promise."

"Thanks." Yunah smiles. "I'll see you soon. I love you."

"I love you, too, Yunah-ya," her mother says.

"Me too!" her father says from afar. Yunah chuckles to herself.

The call ends and Yunah is already thinking about requesting an extended leave. She figures it is time for a reset, a chance for something new, a way to circumvent this dead end of her life.

She grabs the soju bottle by the neck and takes a deep swig, wiping her mouth afterward.

She types up an email to Cole on her phone, explaining everything precisely as it happened, and presses "Send." She doesn't care about the repercussions. This is the least that Jihoon deserves. He is innocent.

Her grandmother used to carry out jesa for her husband, who passed away before Yunah was born. Yunah's parents had ignored the tradition since leaving Korea, but once her grandmother arrived, she wouldn't let them skip it. She lamented how her husband would be crushed to learn that his family had forgotten him. So she taught Yunah how to do a special bow reserved for jesa. Except it was now so long ago she doesn't quite remember how it went, how many times she needs to bow.

Yunah kneels, puts her hand on top of the other — both of her palms facing down — brings them to the floor, and bows. She's not sure whether her head should go completely to the ground. So instead, she looks at Jihoon. Once she feels that she has stayed like that long enough, she gets up.

•

A week before departing for Oxford, she gets some time off to spend with her family. It is a courtesy from the agency, as she will not be given any vacation time while on assignment. She thought she would relax, perhaps catch up on lost time with her mother and father, but she quickly was reminded why she doesn't visit home much in the first place.

"So, are you seeing anyone right now?" her mother says at their first dinner together.

"No."

"Yunah-ya. This is a real problem, you know?"

"Why is it a problem?"

"You don't see that it's a problem?"

"Yeobo, please, she doesn't want to talk about it," her father says.

Her father tries his best to change the topic and talks about their bagel store and then about church. The discussion soon turns into church gossip and Yunah's mother starts to badmouth a few of the parishioners. "The disrespect of that woman! I'm an elder now," she exclaims.

Yunah silently thanks her father for the distraction. Church is the one topic guaranteed to turn her mother's attention away from anything. She loves to gossip and the only source is from church.

"How long are you going to be in Oxford?" her father asks.

"They say two years, maybe more."

"Two?" Her mother stops in the middle of picking up strands of seasoned bean sprouts. "Two years? You'll be pushing thirty!"

"And?"

"How does this — When are you —" she seems to be stumped, until finally she sets her chopsticks down. "Yunah-ya, I know all this work is important to you, but when are you going to find a husband?"

"Eomma, that's not up to you. I'll find someone when I do, but even if I never find someone, that's my business."

"How is it not my business? You potentially ending up alone? That's not what I wish for you."

"And I'm saying that I don't care."

"Yunah-ya, do you know how hard it is for a woman in her thirties to find a man to marry, to have a family with?"

"I do plenty well on my own, Eomma. Can you get off my case?"

Her mother does not respond. They finish the meal in silence, and when Yunah rises to help clean up, her mother curtly says, "Don't bother."

"Come on. Let's go for a walk," her father says, pulling her lightly by the arm toward the door.

Outside, she sees that the neighbourhood has not changed much. From the damp night air to the way the streetlights shine down on the road, it's all the same. They go down the pathway where she used to jog when she was training for track. She would run all the way to the nearby baseball park, where she did her laps before returning home.

"Eomma finally made elder at church?" Yunah asks.

"Yeah, she's been happy about that."

"Apparently not happy enough to leave me alone."

"She's just worried, that's all."

"My dating life is something for me to worry about. I just haven't found anyone I like."

Her father seems to ponder this, then asks, "What are you looking for?"

Yunah thinks back to all the men she dated. One was in freshman year, an older Korean student who expected her to reciprocate expensive meals with sexual favours. Another was a Qatari international student who tried to kiss her in his BMW, to which she responded by pulling away. He was so confused, not understanding why his car had not aroused her. During sophomore year, there was the long-haired man from the Midwest who had been to China the summer before. It ended after a few months: he found her far too confident and self-assured for a real Asian woman. And after a few more of these duds throughout her university years, she eventually stopped looking because she found all of it pointless.

"I've looked, Appa. I don't think I'll ever meet anybody."

"Yunah-ya, you can still find someone. It doesn't have to result in marriage or children. It can be a companion, a partner with whom you can share the ups and downs of life."

"Is that how you have it with Eomma?"

"Yes. We are partners. We came to this country with only each other. And we made a place for ourselves here. What we have, the bond that we share, sustains us. It sustained you."

"Appa, I don't need a partner."

"Yunah-ya," her father says, taking the tone he often uses when he is about to give a lecture. "You've done so well with your life so far. But in the end, you need someone to share your life with. You need someone who understands you, who shares the burden of suffering with you."

"Is Eomma that person for you?"

"More or less," he chuckles.

They walk back to the house. Before she opens the door, she feels like this is her last chance, at least for a while, to ask the one thing she has wondered for so long. "Did you two stay together because of me?"

"What?"

"When the bagel shop almost failed, Eomma was talking about how she wanted to go back to Korea, and you wanted to stay because there was nothing back there for you. I heard you fighting about it every day. I couldn't go to school in the morning without hearing her grumbling about how she was sick of it all. Then I got the acceptance letter to Harvard and suddenly everything was better. What happened, exactly?"

Her father scratches the side of his head. He turns to Yunah, but then turns away, and he does this a few times before he finally settles. "When you got that letter, we went to church right away. We thanked God for the good fortune and for giving us the strength to go on in this strange place. And after that, we knew we could not give up on each other. Watching you achieve greatness like that — it was as if the world was telling us, yes, there is a reward at the end of all this. It was worth it for us to hold on. It was all worth it in the end."

Yunah wonders about what could have happened if she had never got into Harvard. If it would have all broken apart because she got into a second-rate school instead. What words would they be exchanging then? Would they even still be together like this?

"Yunah-ya," he says. "Someday you'll understand. When you're older, when your heart grows tired. Time gets to us all. I know you don't want to listen now, but you'll get it one day."

But what he doesn't mention is that her parents have become each other's prison. It's obvious to Yunah. In making the daring leap across the world, they have now become each other's only option for ally. Yunah would rather be alone than put up with someone in such a way, to gradually dig a trench between her and a partner because they can neither separate nor be together. She wants someone to share her truth with. And if no one can do that with her, she'd rather go it alone.

The Nameless

Just as the Soju Club comes into view, Yohan sees Seonhye outside with a lighter in one hand and a cigarette between her lips, staring at him as he turns off the motorbike and dismounts. When the surprise seems to dissipate, she takes the cigarette out of her mouth.

"I ran into your friends." Yohan points toward where he came from. "They're on Headington. I called an ambulance for them."

"Ambulance?" she says, seemingly ruminating on this. "Well, that's more of my people in the hospital then."

Then, she starts giggling. It gets more intense, until she has broken out into raucous laughter. "What a fucking shitshow," she exclaims into the sky.

When she calms down, she adds, "Dr. Ryu was here. You're late."

Soju Club, Dr. Ryu. Doha's orders proved to be correct.

"Where is she now?"

"Let me recall. We were in a standoff, and I had things under control, but your boss just decided to give herself up. Something about letting you go and handing herself over instead," Seonhye says nonchalantly before she lights the cigarette and takes the first puff. "Why did you even come back? Didn't she tell you to leave?"

"I can't just leave."

"Sure you can. You could've left just now. Yet you're back."

"If you were me, where would you go?" he asks.

"If I were you? Depends. I'd go somewhere quiet, where people won't ask too many questions. A small place but not too small. You don't want to be in a place where everyone knows everyone. It's harder to be anonymous. And I don't see you as someone who'd get along well with others."

"I get along with others."

She laughs. "But you don't. You just sort of slide in and don't say much, then slide out when it's time for you to go. That's not getting along. That's just being there, hoping no one notices you."

"We get along."

"We get along because it was my job to watch you and get along with you, and it was also your job to not make trouble. Our professional obligations overlapped," she says as she weaves her fingers together to demonstrate. "Thus, we manufactured a friendship."

"So all of it was fake?"

"Okay, let's cut the crap," she says, shaking her head. "There is no Seonhye Park, but you knew that already. Yet you still came to the Magpie. All of this was a game of lies. And what does it matter? I'm leaving, you're leaving. We're not gonna see each other again. We had jobs to do and our paths crossed. What more do you want? You got your freedom, didn't you? I have to go back home and face God knows what."

For a while, Yohan watches Seonhye, or the woman who is pretending to be Seonhye, smoke in silence. Her cigarette soon gets to the end of the filter, which she drops on the ground and snuffs out with her heel. "Well," she says. "That's it. You should be on your way. I won't tell anyone. Have a good life."

She starts to walk away, but before she is out of earshot, Yohan calls out to her. "Wait." She turns around and spreads her arms, as if to tell him that she hasn't got all day.

"I'm Yohan. Kim Yohan. I don't know where I'm really from. Dr. Ryu and Doha took me in. I've been with them since I was a child."

She comes back to him, looking intrigued. She pulls out the pack of smokes and takes out two cigarettes. One goes to her mouth and the other is offered to Yohan, who takes it. She flicks on the lighter and he leans in to put the tip of his cigarette into the flame. They both take the first puffs, the smoke filling the night air between them.

"Yohan," she says slowly, saying each syllable with deliberation. "Kim Yohan. That's who you are?"

"You didn't know?"

She shakes her head. "I'm Yunah. Yunah Choi. Or as you say, Choi Yunah. I was born in Nassau, Long Island. Jericho to be exact. My parents own a bagel store. I worked there during the summers, so I know how to cut a bagel properly."

"And what's the proper way to cut a bagel?"

"You press down on it flat," she says as she holds out her hand, palm facing the ground. "Then you find the midpoint with the breadknife and just slice through beneath your palm. It makes a cleaner cut and it's faster."

"Yunah. I like the name."

She smiles at him.

Yohan takes one last drag on the cigarette and then tosses it onto the ground. Yunah does the same.

"Help me," he says.

"Help you with what?"

"Get her back."

"Forget it. Why would I risk myself like that?"

"You can bring me in. Me for her life."

Yunah laughs. "Funny, she suggested the same thing. Her life for your freedom. Why don't you listen to your boss and get out of here? What is any of this to you? Is it loyalty? Fuck all of that. Just leave. She's even telling you to leave."

"I can't just leave. I have to try something because I should have been with him when it happened. I should've been there by his side. To defend him. I'm not going to make that mistake again with her."

She looks at him, her eyes softer. "What are they to you?"

"I don't know," he says, shaking his head.

"You don't want to lose her. That's it, right?"

"Yes."

"It sounds like you love them. That's what it means when you don't want to lose them."

He takes a moment to register her words. She holds out a hand. Yohan grabs it and they do a light but firm shake.

"Okay," she says. "It's a deal."

CHAPTER 11

The Exiled

THE OPERATIVE HAS BEEN WATCHING DOHA AND LETS me know that he is now near the square. I tell him to hold off and to watch for anyone approaching the area. I step out of the café and go toward Doha, who is right by Carfax Tower. When I get there, there is a throng of tourists trying to take pictures, and to the side, there is Doha, looking around until he sees me coming. He is glad to see me, and I am glad to see him as well.

I lead him into a secluded alleyway nearby that I had staked out earlier, and when we are hidden from view, we embrace.

"Been a while, hasn't it?" Doha asks.

"Yes, it has been."

"You look tired."

"Hasn't been exactly easy hunting them all down. Almost forgot how well we trained them all."

"We did good work."

"Yes, we did indeed."

We chuckle and it almost feels as if everything is as it used to be, before the regime change, before the order. But of course, we can never go back. We can't keep any of what we have built. It all must be erased. The new Leader wants a clean slate.

"How is Yohan?" I ask.

"Slightly confused, but he doesn't say."

"Does he know?"

"No, he does not know any of this."

"Good, we meant for him to be in the dark. He will never find out what we did for him."

"Yohan should leave as soon as possible. Preferably right now," Doha says.

"I want to wait until I talk to her."

"Seonhye? Or is it Yunah? Tell me, what is your interest in her? Why is she important in all of this?"

"The boy needs to learn. He needs to learn how to exist in a world with others on his own accord. He has only known relationships that are bound by duty rather than choice. He yearns for it. I saw it when he botched Paris. He wants to connect, but we never gave him that."

"What about us?" Doha says, putting his hand on his chest. "We love him, right?"

I stop and stare at him. I always knew that Doha held Yohan in a special place in his heart, though he never expressed it. In a program filled with agents either frequently getting killed or deserting, Yohan's longevity was a result of close care by Doha. It is why Yohan is the only one who lives with Doha in Oxford.

"He needs to be able to choose. He never chose us. We chose him."

"I see," Doha says. I hear a tinge of sadness in his tone.

"Don't be like that. We're almost there."

Doha looks down, his eyes closed. When he looks back up, I can see that his eyes are wet. I present my hand to him, which he takes. I feel a gentle squeeze from him.

"I've made the necessary arrangements," Doha says. "The South Koreans, the Americans, they have all been alerted. I see them around. Closely monitoring, watching. They know we're here. They know something is happening. So let's keep them guessing. Let's keep them running around in circles."

I nod.

"The operative assigned to you. Does he know?" he asks.

"He will do as I say."

"Are you sure he is trustworthy?"

"It's going to be fine, Doha. He will be fine. You worry too much. This isn't like you. We'll try to meet at the Soju Club, like you asked. It will be fine as long as he knows that he must stay in Oxford until I can safely extract him."

Doha's face relaxes. "You are right. And he'll feel at home at the Soju Club. He can have one last drink."

"You and your drinks. Why the Soju Club?"

"It's our place."

"It used to be our place," I say.

"Until the owner sold it off."

We share a brief laugh, reminded of our youthful nights in Oxford.

"I will try to meet him there, but I can't guarantee it. You know how it is. There are no certainties in this business."

"Of course. I trust you," he says with a grin, his lips upturned to one side.

I smile back, but it quickly fades, knowing what needs to happen.

"Now do it."

I take out a switchblade. I have imagined it repeatedly, trying to picture my hand as the knife sinks into his skin and flesh. The way it bucks against the push of my thrust. Every single time, I shudder at the scene. For a moment, I want to convince him otherwise.

"Do it," he says, looking at me.

I realize that Doha's fate was sealed from the start. As a bastard Kim pushed out of the competition for the throne, he would never be able to escape his origins. For all his life, he was in a state of limbo, floating along with no destination. But I step back and hesitate.

"Please," he says. "I don't want to be killed by some thug they send." He unbuttons his coat and pulls it aside to reveal his shirt beneath. I take a few long breaths to steady my nerves. "Under the rib, in the middle. You know where, right?"

I nod and get in close. I thrust the knife in. He sucks in his breath hard and his lips tremble as he grunts from the pain. I hold him up with my one free arm, and the weight of his body pulls me down with him. He gasps as he falls to his knees. I kneel with him, embracing him, until he collapses.

I pull out the blade and wipe my bloodied hand on my coat. His breathing quickens, and the realization of what I have just done hits me. I wonder if it is too late to turn back. Could I call for an ambulance and save him? I hear a rumble get closer and see the agent on his motorcycle.

"We need to go. Yohan is on the move. He's been tracking Doha."

I climb on the back of the bike and take one last look at Doha. He is looking back at me, and we share a brief moment before the motorcycle speeds away from the alleyway. The night blurs as tears flood my eyes.

The Rejected

They stop in the middle of the road adjacent to Abingdon Airfield. It is a private airfield, unlit at this time of the night, and there are no planes in sight except a small white Cessna jet waiting on the tarmac.

"That's it, that's the plane." Yohan points to it.

Next to the plane is the black Volkswagen Golf. Yunah and Yohan dismount the motorbike and approach the fence. From the edge of the airfield, they observe a figure carrying a bag out of the trunk and then up the ramp onto the plane.

"This thing." She pulls out her Glock 42. "Effective up to maybe twenty-five metres — that is, if I get my shots in perfectly. So I need to really get in close."

Between the two of them, this is all the firepower they have. The risk is great, but the reward could be greater. She can bring both Yohan and Dr. Ryu in, and that will be more than enough. She will have accomplished her mission despite today's mess.

"How do we approach him? There's no cover," Yohan asks.

Yunah takes another look at the airfield. There is nothing but open tarmac. She checks the magazine of her peashooter: she has three shots left. She needs time to get close and she has an idea. "Distract him with the motorcycle."

Yohan understands immediately. "I'll draw his fire. You approach from the side."

"A pincer," Yunah says, holding up a V with her fingers.

"Get as close as you can without drawing any attention. When you see me riding in, that's your cue to sprint as fast as you can until you have your shot."

She puts her hand on his back. "Good luck."

"You too," he says.

They exchange a look. He nods and she nods back. Yohan rides away with his headlight off, following the road that loops around the airfield. Yunah tucks her gun in her hip and hops over the low wire fence. She starts to approach, keeping herself low. She sees Deoksu pull Dr. Ryu out of the car, handcuffed with her arms in front. Yunah quickens her pace. There is not much time.

When she is about half a kilometre away, she hears the roar of the café racer echo on the runway. With a single beam of headlight focused on the car, Yohan's motorcycle charges in. This immediately draws Deoksu's attention. He raises his gun to take aim at Yohan. As Yunah starts to sprint toward Deoksu, she hears a shot and sees Yohan changing his course, skidding into a sharp turn, and then going the other way. Behind the cover of the Volkswagen, Deoksu follows the bike with discipline, cracking shots one by one.

Sparks flash as the motorcycle falls to the ground, sliding on its side, sending Yohan tumbling onto the tarmac. Yunah is still too far away, perhaps a little less than a hundred metres. She sees Yohan in the distance, crawling to the bike for cover as bits of asphalt kick up around him from Deoksu continuing to fire at him. Desperate, Yunah stops, takes aim, and shoots. She misses completely and Deoksu does not even notice.

Yunah dashes closer as Yohan keeps as low as possible while pinned by gunfire. When she thinks she is in a good range, she takes aim and shoots again. This time she manages to hit Deoksu in the left shoulder. He jerks backward and falls.

"Stay down. Don't, don't!" she shouts. Only a few metres away, Yunah keeps her sight trained on Deoksu's head. Dr. Ryu is crouched behind the car, keeping herself as small as possible.

"Drop it!" Yunah tells him.

He glares up at her as he clutches his wounded shoulder, his gun still in hand but touching the ground. "Fuck you," he says. "Fuck you, you American piece of shit. You're the worst of them all. Going around, pretending to be one of us just because you look like us, but you're not like us. You're not Korean. You don't have an ounce of who we are in you."

Yunah keeps her gun trained on him.

"You're just like them. Coming around, messing up everyone's plans, thinking you're better. But you aren't. You don't deserve to win. You don't deserve anything."

"Drop the gun."

"He's dead because of you. Jihoon is dead because of you and your American morons running all over the place."

Her eyes twitch at the mention of Jihoon. "Just drop the gun."

"Ssibal-nyeon. I should've killed you back there."

Deoksu seems to ease his grip on his gun, wincing in pain as he holds his shoulder close, but he suddenly grunts and raises the weapon. Yunah sees his hand contract. She fires the last round into his forehead just as he sends one into her body.

•

Junichi comes to the Magpie regularly after that second night. Command thinks it is a sign that the operation is going well, and they prod her to ask him questions, push him on details. But Yunah finds it premature. She needs to make sure that he is comfortable with her. That has not happened yet, as far as she can tell.

"Do you travel much?" she asks him once she feels like she has built enough rapport to pry a little more.

"No, I rarely leave town."

This is a lie, as she knows he has gone to multiple locations across the continent. Most recently to Bergen, where there was a mysterious suicide of a man. When they dispatched an agent there, they found the body to be that of an Asian restaurant worker who went missing months before in Berlin but was unreported because he had overstayed on an expired visa. They suspect that this body is a decoy. She wants to ask about it. Thinking about how to engage him into more talk, she brings out another old-fashioned onto the bar for him once he is finished with his last drink.

"Do you talk to your folks back home often?" he asks.

"Not really."

"Why?"

"I mean, I kind of came out here to get away from them."

"You don't like them?" Junichi's eyes widen. He seems to be genuinely surprised at this.

"No, it's not that. I just need some room, you know?"

"I see." Junichi looks down at his drink for a few seconds, then continues. "Growing up, my parents were busy all the time. I rarely saw them. They were always travelling or working. So I was raised by other people, you know? Nannies and all that. After that I went to a boarding school. So I got to see them even less then."

"You've turned out so well, though. Come on," Yunah says as playfully as she can.

"I don't know. I just look at other people and think about what it's like. To have real parents. Not just someone you share a space with, but someone who takes care of you. Always looks out for you. Doesn't matter if you've been gone for a long time. Whenever you come back, they're happy to see you."

"Junichi, please, every parent is happy to see their child, so don't say your parents are not like that. They just show their love differently."

"I get that, but I just feel like there's always a distance I can't cross."

Yunah thinks about her parents, what they have done for her over the years. During summers when she came back home from university, her mother cooked all her favourite Korean dishes. It didn't matter how busy it got at the bagel store. Her mother always made time to feed Yunah . On birthdays they would never forget to send a card and a gift, usually in the form of money. Yunah wished they would stop. It was risky to send cash by mail.

"Things can be worse, you know," Yunah says. "There are orphans."

"I had a friend who was raised in an orphanage. Didn't know who his parents were. He didn't say much about it. But from what it sounded like, it was bad. Constantly hungry, constantly afraid. Never knew what tomorrow would bring. So you're right, Seonhye. At least I had parents."

A pause lingers as they both take a drink.

"What happened to your friend?" she asks.

"He got out, went to school. Probably has a job now. I haven't seen him in a while."

Perhaps he is talking about a friend, but Yunah senses that it is more than that. It's the way he spoke. A tinge of intimate sadness that could not have come from talking about someone else's pain. She knows she has broken through a barrier. Later that night, she reports this to Cole.

"That's a useless lead," her superior says in an impatient tone. "It has no strategic value. So what if he might have been an orphan and was hungry. Who gives a shit?"

Nevertheless Yunah writes it down and remembers it for all their future conversations. It never comes up again, but in the back of her mind, she now knows he has never known the love of a family. She cannot imagine in what world that wouldn't matter.

The Nameless

When the shooting stops, Yohan peers over the motorcycle. He stands up and starts walking toward the Volkswagen. There is a brief exchange of words between Yunah and Deoksu that he cannot quite make out, followed by gunshots. Yohan runs to the scene. Yunah is writhing on the ground and Deoksu has a hole in his head. He drags Yunah to the side of the car, propping her up so she is sitting.

"Did I get him?" she asks, her breathing heavy.

"You did," Yohan says as he checks her wound. She has been hit in the chest.

"Forget it, gah —" she winces. "Ssibal." Her eyes flutter as she struggles to keep herself from fading. "Do me one favour. Pull out the cigarettes in my jacket and light me one, please."

He reaches into her blood-soaked jacket pocket and takes a cigarette out of the pack, puts it in her waiting mouth, and lights it as she sucks it in deeply.

"You can keep the rest." She points with her chin to the pack, which Yohan puts in his pocket.

Yunah coughs, and Yohan gently pulls the cigarette out of her mouth until her coughing stops. Then he puts the smoke back in between her lips, watching her inhale and close her eyes as nicotine flushes into her body. She shudders, exhaling in staccato.

"Why did you keep coming to the Magpie?" She asks. "You knew what we were. Why put yourself out in the open like that?"

"I liked talking with you."

She smiles and then coughs again. "Same."

As Yunah takes a long drag on the cigarette, Yohan looks around and spots Dr. Ryu going over to Deoksu's body. She digs through his pockets and finds a knife to cut away her ties.

Yohan feels a hand on his wrist and turns his head back to Yunah.

"My parents' bagel place, it's called Choi's Bagel 'cause Choi's sounds like choice, you know? It's kinda smart. My dad thought of it. Get the everything bagel. Have it with the cinnamon cream cheese. It's a great combo. You won't regret it."

"I will."

"Ask for Mr. Choi. That's my dad. He's a nice guy."

"I'll ask for him."

"If you're lucky, my mom will be there too. She doesn't come in as often as she used to. She's got hip problems now."

"Right."

"If you do meet them, don't talk about me. Please."

"I won't."

"They'll feel it was their fault. They don't need to be reminded of me."

"I understand."

He waits until her breathing stops. Her fingers fall from his arm. The cigarette drops from her mouth and goes out on its own in the cold night air. Her head sags to the side, her eyes open without focus and her jaw hanging. Yohan closes her mouth and her eyes. He gently lays her body down on the tarmac, his palm behind her head, so it looks as if she is sleeping. He kneels by her side and holds her hand, still warm. He stares into her face so he can remember it forever. "Goodbye, Choi Yunah."

Yohan struggles to leave Yunah's side. Dr. Ryu comes and pats his shoulder. "We need to leave." She is holding Deoksu's gun in one hand.

Only then does he allow himself to get up. The Volkswagen has been beaten up and shot at, but the car still works.

"Bristol," she says.

CHAPTER 12

The Exiled

I DRIVE OUT TO THE MOUNTAINS NEAR WONSAN, WITH the boy seated next to me. He seems quiet, his head on his hand as he watches the mountain range in the distance slowly passing by. The first time he was in a car was when I finally came to take him away from the orphanage. Delight filled his eyes as I opened the door to the passenger seat to let him jump in. He held his head out the opened window, lost in the winds, his hair waving.

•

When I drive into a clearing, Doha is already there waiting, leaning against his own car, a black Toyota sedan, something he had to fight for when they tried to get him a chauffeur to drive him around. We all walk along an unmarked path through the forest until we come across a small patch of land where a house once stood. There is a small grave, a mound of grass rising perhaps a metre above the ground.

It is an annual ritual. Visiting the grave and doing a modest jesa with a bottle of soju and some fruit. I lay out a cloth in front of the grave and pile apples and clementines into a small pyramid so that it looks somewhat like a jesa table. The boy and I bow together. First we kneel with our hands layered in front of us. Then we bow with palms facing down, our foreheads touching the top of our hands. We stand back up and then repeat for a second time.

Doha hangs back, watching us. When we are done bowing, I pour two glasses of soju and hand one to the boy. We go around to either side, watering the grass on the grave with soju. I turn to the boy. "Would you help me, dear? Can you pick out the weeds here?"

The boy dutifully nods and starts to pull out the weeds by the roots.

Doha takes out a folded paper from his jacket and passes it to me. I read it and see that the boy has been cleared to attend the school we have chosen. The one that guarantees his future and beyond. Even the elites of the North would kill for this piece of paper.

"I just need his name here," he says, pointing at the blank section on the paper. "And then he's in."

"I haven't thought of a name yet," I say, looking at the boy, who is busy picking at weeds. His hair is a mess from the back, and I remind myself to give him a haircut when we're back home. Work has been difficult. The famine is dragging on, and I've been called to many places to deal with more problems and situations.

"I'm off again soon; it'll be for a while," Doha says.

"How long?"

"A year this time. Prague."

"But you just got back."

"Jong-il hyung-nim wants it done, and if I'm to stay in his good graces, I have to be an obedient dog. For his sake at least." Doha flicks his head toward the boy.

"Right."

"And my mother's sake, obviously."

"How is your mother?"

"A day closer to death. I can't wait until she dies so I can truly fuck off."

I know he doesn't mean it. Doha loves his mother. He always comes back from abroad bearing opulent gifts for her. Coats, bags, dresses — his mother's closet is full of luxury brands. She is his only anchor to this place. When she inevitably passes away, so will his loyalty.

"Make sure he studies hard," he says.

"I will."

"And make sure he eats well and stays healthy."

"Of course."

"Will you ever tell him?"

"Tell him about her?"

"Everything. All of it. It'll be cruel not to tell him."

"Wouldn't it be cruel to do so?"

"We all deserve to know who we are, where we came from, don't we?"

"What good will it do to tell him?" I ask.

"He'll wonder. He'll see the gaps. He'll crave a mother. Just like how I craved a father."

"Maybe someday," I mutter. I don't know when that will be because I certainly cannot bear to tell him that beneath his feet is the body of the woman who gave birth to him. That I showed up with a firing squad at his home, a small modest place in the countryside, when he was just a small child. And the only reason his mother was dragged out and shot was that she was not from this country but was a Zainichi Korean, a Korean who migrated back from Japan.

The new Great Leader did not like that sliver of foreignness in her or the fact that she was his father's last consort. As blood pooled around her on the ground, her body tied up in ropes, I looked through the house and found the boy sleeping in the closet. I could not bear to call on the lieutenant to finish the job. I took him and left him at the nearest orphanage, giving the manager a year's salary as goodwill to ensure that the boy would survive.

This is where he used to live. This is where his mother was shot and buried. It was only much later that I put this mound of soil on top of her grave to make it look proper.

Once the boy is done weeding the grave, he walks over to us, and we both smile at him.

"She will be happy that you cleaned her home nicely," I say.

He nods, a faint smile appearing on his face as he looks on his work.

I'm not sure whether I will tell him that this is not my sister's grave and I never had a sister in my entire life. One day I may let him know that this grief that I put on in the form of this annual ritual is, in fact, his.

The Nameless

The sun is coming up and the sky gets brighter as they drive along the coast. She spots a marina nearby and they stop, but before they exit the car, Yohan asks for a small measure of truth from Dr. Ryu.

"Ask it, whatever it is," she says in Korean, a rarity for the two of them.

"Why did he have to die? Doha."

Dr. Ryu lets out a long sigh. "Same reason why all of us perish out here at some point. Home no longer needs us."

He has known this all along, but hearing it confirmed by Dr. Ryu puts a weight on his heart. "Was it you?"

Dr. Ryu looks down at her hands. "Yes."

"Did he know?"

"Yes, he said he would prefer it to be me."

"I see."

Dr. Ryu reaches for his hand and squeezes it gently. "But that won't be your path, Yohan. You will live. Doha and I, we made a pact. That we would get you out no matter what."

With this Yohan has nothing more to say. How Doha lived and how he died, it was never going to be within his control.

"Come, it's time," Dr. Ryu says and gets out of the car.

They walk along a pier until they come across a small white boat. "This is it," she says.

The boat, with a motor in the back, has two seats. She passes him the keys to the boat before removing her ID cards from her wallet and tossing them away. Yohan flips his backpack upside down, emptying passports and documents into the water. He watches them float briefly before they are soaked through and sink into the dark depths beneath. Dr. Ryu then takes out Deoksu's pistol, pops out the magazine, and drops the bullets into the water, except for one.

"What are you doing?" he asks.

"It's all I need," she says.

Yohan, confused, tips his head and frowns. "What do you mean?"

"It's the end for me here."

"Wait," Yohan says, a sudden feeling of desperation creeping up on him. "You're not going to come with me?"

"No, Yohan. It's just you."

"But why?"

Dr. Ryu slowly shakes her head, casting her eyes downward. "Yohan, the republic does not forget. You know this. They'll find me no matter how long or how many people it takes."

"And they'll forget me?"

"They already have. I made sure of it."

"How?"

"Because Yohan Kim does not exist anymore. In fact, he hasn't for quite a while. When you left the country, we destroyed your paper trail. They'll go through the files and never know that you even existed. You were never in North Korea. Right now you are closer to being Junichi Nakamura than Yohan Kim."

Yohan looks down, processing what he has just heard. "So am I still Yohan?"

"You are, if you choose to be."

Dr. Ryu is reminded of something and opens her handbag. "Here, for you, when you are somewhere safe," she says, handing him a small envelope the size of a credit card. Yohan takes it.

Yohan wants to convince her to fight to stay in this world, but he sees the resolve in her eyes. He hugs her, and she wraps her arms around him, one hand behind his head. After a few moments, he backs away gently, gives her one last nod, and gets in the boat. He inserts the key and the boat putters into life. He grabs the handle and steers out to sea. Minutes later he hears a shot crack through the wind, but he does not look back. Instead, he looks up at the grey sky and a drop of water splashes into his eye. The rain gradually dots the water around the boat until it starts to pour. Yohan is soaked and he occasionally wipes his face to see where he is going. But he does not know where he is going.

After two hours he comes across an island. He stops the boat by a wooden pier, ties it up, and then walks along the shore. He looks back out at the sea and wonders if this is where he should be or if he should go elsewhere. He feels a chill and a sense of unease. He takes out Yunah's pack of cigarettes and sees that there are only two left.

From behind he hears footsteps. Yohan whips back, tense on his heels. He sees a man in a red-and-black flannel shirt, with a thick mustache. Upon a closer look, Yohan sees how the man's skin is worn from years of sun, wrinkled and dry. A sheepdog is trailing him. It runs up to Yohan to sniff his hand before dashing back to its owner.

"Excuse me?" he says in a thick accent that Yohan cannot quite place. "Do you mind if I get one off you?"

Without a word, Yohan takes the two cigarettes out and passes one to the man.

"Thanks, mate. What's your name?"

"Yohan," he says. "Yohan Kim."

"Yohan, as in short for Johannes?"

"No, just Yohan. With a *y*."

"Are you Korean? Kim, right? That's Korean."

Yohan thinks for a moment and says, "It's just a name."

When he realizes that he doesn't have a lighter, the man passes his own after he's done with it. Yohan thanks him, flicks it on, burns the end of his cigarette, and then gives it back.

"It's a smooth one," the man remarks. "What is it?"

"THIS."

"Yeah, this cigarette, what is it?"

"THIS," Yohan says and turns the front of the empty cigarette pack toward him.

"Fuck me," he says, laughing. "That's brilliant. Where's it from?"

"A friend gave it to me," Yohan says. "From somewhere far."

"Bummer. Would love to get another one."

Once they are done, the man thanks him again and continues on his walk. Yohan stays a while and watches the waves come and go. He remembers the small envelope. He carefully opens it without making any tears. Inside is a Polaroid of Doha and Dr. Ryu when they were young. Around the same age Yohan is now. They are smiling and in front of the Radcliffe Camera in Oxford.

He can tell they are happy. Inexplicably and undeniably happy.

For a moment, he thinks about throwing the photo into the water, but he changes his mind and tucks it into the now empty pack of cigarettes and puts it all back inside his coat. Once he is ready, he turns around. In the distance he can still see the man walking up the trail. His dog stops and looks at Yohan, as if asking for him to follow. Perhaps there is a village nearby. A place to find food and rest, where he can lay his body down and think about tomorrow and all the days after that.

With his empty backpack over his shoulder, he walks toward the dog, behind which the morning sun has risen high.

Live. Yohan-a. Live.

So he will live.

END

Acknowledgements

MY SINCERE AND HEARTFELT THANKS TO:

Sarah. On an autumn day during a car ride to your parents' place, I told you about a book idea I had. You were so thrilled about it, especially about how great the title sounded. Your nudge was what started it all. I can go on and on about all the small and big ways you have supported my writing, whether it was reading the book's most embarrassing versions and giving feedback, or allowing me the space to write when life was at its most breakneck pace.

Julia Kim. Just when I was about to put this book away in the proverbial drawer, you popped a DM in TikTok and introduced yourself as an editor with interest in the book, reigniting my hope again. Your guidance and editorial eye sculpted the book into its best shape. Without you, it would have just collected digital dust.

Everyone at the Asian Canadian Writers' Workshop. The ACWW's Jim Wong-Chu Emerging Writers Award gave me the first serious literary validation for *Oxford Soju Club*, and also convinced me that my writing was worthy of being read as a novel.

Claude Lalumière. My first writing teacher and the person who gave me the courage and motivation to keep writing. You were the first one to tell me that my writing had potential.

Amal Chatterjee. My supervisor at Oxford and my mentor throughout the years. Whenever I was at my wit's ends about what to do, whether continuing my writerly journey was worth it or not, you were always there to lend your wisdom.

Anton Hur and Janet Hong for being the literary seonbaes that I needed at the right time. Your advice and counsel have righted my ship more times than I can count.

My friends from my master's program at Oxford. Our time together during our study, as well as afterward, has taught me so much about what kind of writer I need to become. Many of you stepped forward when I needed help with this book when you were all busy with your own lives. Our camaraderie is the best thing that I have taken from the degree.

The entire team at Dundurn Press. You've stewarded this book to publication with passion and professionalism. You've always welcomed my suggestions and ideas, and I've learned with you what it truly means to have constructive collaboration on a novel. The lessons I've taken from this process will surely help me throughout my entire career.

My dear friends who have read this book and didn't shy away from giving their honest thoughts. My first and foremost goal with this book was to write something that would be fun for the closest people around me. It was a joy to hear what worked and what didn't. Particularly Hyeree, Ruxandra, Yasmine, Laurence, and An. Your feedback was crucial when this book was rougher than sandpaper.

My sister. For being a staunch believer in my writing career. Whenever it seemed like I was not going to be able to do this thing, you helped me to stand back up and told me to keep going. No matter how ridiculous the idea is, you are always willing to listen and share your thoughts with glee.

My mother and father. When we were fresh immigrants and I was about to enter elementary school, I was embarrassed about my weak English. But you told me instead to feel pride for my excellent Korean. You've instilled in me steadfast self-esteem in my cultural heritage, and that is the reason why I am now proudly and unabashedly Korean.

And finally, Noah. This book was my attempt at deciphering the lifelong question of trying to discover who I truly was beneath the layers of different identities and selves I had accumulated. When you were born, I found new answers to my mission, and that in turn I poured into this book.

About the Author

JINWOO PARK is a Korean Canadian writer based in Montreal. Born and raised in Seoul, he has lived in various parts of North America and the U.K. since the age of eleven.

He obtained his bachelor's degree from McGill University in 2013, followed by a master's in political economics from the London School of Economics in 2014, and a master's in creative writing at the University of Oxford in 2015. Since graduation, Park has held various jobs in tech companies, marketing agencies, and game studios.

In 2021, he won the Jim Wong-Chu Emerging Writers Award for his first manuscript, *Oxford Soju Club*. Besides his writing career, he has been actively working as a literary translator after winning the LTI Korea Translation Award for Aspiring Translators in late 2023. He is an editor for *Ricepaper* magazine.

He is also an avid book reviewer and is active on TikTok, Instagram, and YouTube.